ONCE UPON A CRIME

WATERFELL TWEED COZY MYSTERY SERIES:
BOOK ONE

MONA MARPLE

For S

Thank you for your constant belief in me

1

*I*t was a bitter day in Waterfell Tweed.

Woken by the hammering rain earlier than she'd like, Sandy got herself ready in a rush. She had spent an hour devouring her latest mystery novel before spotting the time. She was often left with little time to get ready because of her love for books! She pulled on her bright yellow mac and braved the day.

The rain attacked her, hitting her with an almost horizontal angle thanks to the wind. The village's elevated position meant the wind was too common.

Sandy didn't mind rain, especially if she had the choice of curling up inside with a big mug of mocha. But wind? It seemed so pointless.

"Good morning!" a cheery voice called as Sandy unlocked her car door. She turned to see Elaine Peters, her next-door neighbour, being pulled by her dalmatian Scamp as much as the wind itself.

"Morning Elaine, great weather," Sandy called.

Elaine laughed as if she had heard the funniest joke of

the year, which it may have been to her. Elaine kept herself
to herself; had done ever since her husband had died.

"Have a lovely day," Elaine said. "I'll pop down later for
your thing."

"Thank you!" Sandy called and climbed in the old Land
Rover. She hadn't expected Elaine to show her face at the
fundraiser.

Sandy's drive to Books and Bakes took just under five
minutes. The route was a single winding road through the
stunning scenery of the Peak District. She usually turned
off the radio in the car and enjoyed the quiet time with her
thoughts and the view. Lately, she had become more and
more distracted by worries over the shop's declining profits.
It had become hard for her to even notice the pretty countryside as she drove through it.

But today she wouldn't allow those thoughts into
her mind.

Today was the fundraiser. A huge cake sale (and Sandy
hoped books would sell too!) with half of the profits going to
the primary school's collection for roof repairs.

The famous Waterfell Tweed winds had scattered eigh-
teen roof tiles around the playground a fortnight before (on
a Saturday) and, because the winds were 'predictable', the
school insurance had refused to pay out.

Sandy arrived at the shop and parked. She had put her
staff on short hours a month before, meaning she had to
arrive to a shop in darkness each morning and prepare
everything for the day herself.

As she turned the corner this morning, however, and her
shop came into view, her stomach lurched as she saw the
lights on and a fresh stream of (now soaked) bunting
hanging along the window.

She dashed to the door and let herself in, the bell signalling her arrival.

The music was playing and laughter came from the kitchen. She padded across the café seating section and behind the counter, just as a friendly face appeared from the kitchen.

"What time do you call this?" Bernice Alton asked, her red lips breaking into a huge smile.

"Oh, Bernice!" Sandy cried, as her eyes began to water. When Sandy had reduced her employee's hours just weeks before, Bernice had grabbed her hand and told her she'd enjoy a few lie-ins until things improved.

"Come on, no time for that," Bernice said, leading Sandy into the kitchen.

Her oldest friend, who Sandy was sure had never stepped foot in a kitchen before, was mixing a bowl of ingredients. Flour flecks made her hair white in places.

"Cass?"

"Don't faint!" Cass said, splashing more of the cake mixture onto the work surface.

"You guys are amazing. Thank you so much... as soon as things get better..."

"Enough of that. Let's get to work." Bernice said.

Sandy pulled off her mac, washed her hands and surveyed the room. Laid out on trays to cool were chocolate chip and macadamia nut cookies. Sea salt and hazelnut muffins were just being taken out of the oven, and old-fashioned individual apple pies smelt delicious. Bernice and Cass must have been baking for hours.

"What needs doing?"

"I'm on the lemon cake," Cass said, gesturing to the pitiful remainders in the bowl she was mixing.

"There's a coffee and walnut in the oven and I've just put ginger ice cream to freeze," Bernice said.

"Ginger ice cream? Wow." Sandy remarked. Bernice was a creative baker, experimenting with glee over new recipes. Sometimes she just made them up. Sandy much preferred having a tried-and-tested recipe to follow.

"I tasted it, it was awful," Cass said with a laugh.

Bernice raised an eyebrow then swatted Cass' back with a tea towel.

"Hey!" Cass exclaimed. "I'm only sharing my opinion!"

"Let's see how the lemon cake turns out," Bernice said, but she was smiling. She could appear stern but she put that down to her military upbringing. Hers was a home with an abundance of love, she would often say, but no shouting about it.

Sandy shook her head in wonder and allowed her shoulders to relax. It wasn't the life she had expected to live but she wouldn't change things for the world. Well, other than more paying customers so she wasn't scared of opening the bills sometimes.

"Sandy?" Bernice asked, her voice a whisper as Cass disappeared to make herself a fresh cappuccino from behind the shop counter.

"Yeah?"

"Are you ok?" The older woman asked, her eyebrows furrowed.

"I'm fine," Sandy said, forcing a smile. She hated being asked if she was okay, something about the question made her feel as though she might cry even if she'd been happy before hearing the question.

"You seemed jumpy when you got here."

"Oh!" Sandy burst into a laugh. "That! Yes, yes I guess I

was.   I wondered who was in here with the lights on that's all."

"Ooh yes, Jim Slaughter would be no protection if we'd been two armed robbers!" Cass shrieked with laughter from the doorway, a mug of hot cappuccino in her hands.

"Cassandra!" Bernice scolded, with a smile. Jim was the local policeman, and he had more phobias than anyone else Sandy had ever met. His mother had even hinted that he still wouldn't sleep in the dark.

"I wouldn't need Jim anyhow, I can protect myself," Sandy mumbled. Bernice and Cass were chatting among themselves and didn't hear.

**

By the time Books and Bakes opened at 9:05 am because the kitchen clock was a few minutes behind, Sandy was delighted to see a small line formed at the door.

Nothing like a school fundraiser to bring such community together, and it made Sandy's heart swell with pride.

"Good morning!" She called to the wet line of people in rain macs, holding the door open as they dripped rain all over the floor.

"Nothing good about a day this wet." Dorie Slaughter, the village battleaxe and Jim's mum, muttered as she folded her umbrella and traipsed past Sandy.

"Umbrella in the box, please." Sandy reminded.

"In the box?   Another newfangled idea.   What if someone steals it?" Dorie grumbled. At least five people voiced their fear of their tatty umbrellas being stolen every time it rained, to Sandy's amusement.

"I can't imagine anyone will set out without one of their

own today, Dorie. But if the unthinkable happens, you can take my own with you. Okay?"

"Fair enough I guess," Dorie said, lowering herself into the chair closest to the unlit fire. "I'll take a milky coffee and a sausage cob."

"Coming right up," Sandy said with a flourish. Dorie was pleasant beneath her grumbles and a loyal customer. She made a point of trying every new cake and gave honest feedback about which were the nicest. It made Sandy sad to notice she only ever came in alone.

The other customers were browsing around the book-shelves to Sandy's delight. She enjoyed running the cafe side of the business but cakes alone weren't enough to make the business work. When she'd told Cass that she planned to open a cafe and bookshop, her best friend had suggested that she open a nail salon instead. Sandy had laughed; she wasn't a nail salon person. Cass had used her own idea, renting a small shop across the village square and opening LA Nails. Sandy was proud of her friend, but she sometimes looked at the constant stream of customers coming and wished her passion had been for beauty instead of books.

"Do you know, dear..." Dorie called out as Sandy appeared with her plate of food.

"What's that?"

"Well have you heard the news? My James has been casting his net."

"I'm sorry?"

Dorie rolled her eyes. She loved to be the first to share gossip, even when it was about her only son. "He's back on the market. Dating. Quite a catch he is"

"Oh. Wonderful." Sandy said, hoping that Dorie wasn't attempting to match make.

"He won't tell me who she is yet but I remember his sort.

It will be someone glamorous. You homely women would be better for him, but he always goes for looks instead..."

Sandy walked away from Dorie and attempted to not take offence at the woman's words, not that she could deny their truth. She was a homely woman, with a muffin top over her jeans and a double chin. The chin took her by surprise every time she turned her phone camera on selfie mode. But, she was happy. And she didn't want to be Jim Slaughter's type. He was friend material only.

The door opened then and a gust of wind sent Dorie's napkin flying. Sandy moved to grab it and banged heads with the new visitor who had also ducked to retrieve it.

"Oh, darling!" Reginald Halfman cried, cupping his injured head and collapsing into the seat closest to him.

"I'm so sorry! Are you okay?" Sandy asked although she knew he was fine and didn't have much patience for amateur dramatics.

"Yes, love, yes, I shall live to fight another day! An espresso is very much needed, and on the house, I hope. Some people would sue..."

"Oh, Reg..." Sandy said, knowing he hated the abbreviated form. "Give me two minutes."

She returned to the counter and made his drink. Another six customers arrived and, she noted, four of them headed straight for the cafe without even a glance at the bookshelves. The problem, she felt sure, was that the books occupied such a small space within the shop they almost appeared to be an afterthought. Occasionally, customers had even asked her whether they could look at the books!

"Here you go," Sandy said, placing the tiny drink in front of Reginald. He was a tall and trim man with a gleaming bald head and a cutting tongue. He and Dorie eyed each other, enemies of old.

"You, my dear, are an absolute lifesaver." He said, grabbing her hand and squeezing hard.

"Yes, some say. Enjoy."

Sandy approached the next table where a man and woman she didn't know sat shivering in their rain macs. "What can I get for you?"

"Pot of tea please, two cups." The man said.

"Any cakes? Nice bacon cob to warm you up?"

"Ooh no, we only came in to escape the rain." The man said as if paying for tea was frivolous.

"Well you're welcome, and please have a browse of the books to help you stay dry for longer," Sandy said with a smile. "Ladies and gentlemen, friends and enemies alike!" Reginald's flamboyant voice startled Sandy. She turned to see him standing on top of one of her cafe tables!

"Reginald, get down from there. You'll hurt yourself." She called, approaching him.

"Don't be ridiculous, girl, I need to be here to address my public."

"Reginald..."

"Shall I call the police?" Dorie asked, also rising from her chair. "My son is a police officer, ladies and gentlemen. Do not panic."

"Oh Dorothy, be quiet." Reginald said.

"Health and safety will be coming if you get mud all over the tables." The pot-of-tea-man said with a snicker.

"Ladies and gentlemen, I have an announcement, are you ready? It's so exciting!"

Dorie's ears pricked up, and she returned her old Nokia to her handbag.

"I, Reginald Leopold Halfman, can announce that in just seven days' time, I shall take over the business you now know as LA Nails and - drum roll please - transforming it into The Book Stop!"

"What?" Sandy asked.

"Yes! Yes! I will bring culture and intellectual interests to our lovely village. Isn't it exciting!"

"A bookshop? Like mine?" Sandy asked.

"No darling, much bigger! Much better! This place is a wonderful hobby, I'm sure, but imagine what a real businessman could do. I can hardly stand the excitement."

Sandy swallowed and focused her gaze on a spot on the counter to force the tears back. Reginald Halfman was one of the wealthiest people in the village. He would have the funds for stock she couldn't dream of, a full team of staff, authors to attend events... there was no way she could compete with him.

Her business was as good as ruined.

2

*S*andy washed the plates with a heavy spirit, fearing how many more nights she would have standing in this kitchen washing these pots.

The cafe had been busy all day, an endless stream of visitors keeping her busy serving refreshments and cakes and even selling books.

Charlotte Harlow, a pharmaceutical rep originally from the village, bought a beautifully illustrated book of children's poetry, and she didn't even have children.

Elaine Peters had turned up as promised, her eyelashes, like heavy spiders, coated in mascara as she smiled the whole way through her green tea. It was great to watch her taking part in village life again.

Sandy finished rinsing the last dishes and took a stroll before heading home. She wandered through the graveyard and through the grounds of Waterfell Manor. The drizzle had stopped in the morning, so the ground was dry and the temperature nice; with a clear crisp autumn feel to the air that Sandy loved.

She had taken over £1,000 that day, a figure that made

her eyes water. A good part of that would go to the school fund. But just that the numbers were possible would have given Sandy hope she could reach them again, maybe often even. Reginald's news changed everything.

There had been a rumble of energy in the shop ever since his announcement. She'd plastered a smile on her face and hoped she convinced people she felt pleased to see a rival bookstore open just opposite her own.

She was disappointed in Reginald but not surprised. Cass' silence about the plans hurt more. Sandy couldn't understand how her best friend was allowing Reginald to take over her own premises to put Sandy out of business. Cass had rung her four times that afternoon; Sandy stood watching each call come in without answering any.

She would have to face her friend, she knew. But not yet.

**

The hammering at the door woke Sandy from a light nap. She opened her eyes to discover that she had been lying on the settee, still clothed, with the TV still playing. She never fell asleep before 10pm.

She stood and padded across to the front door, pulling her fleece jacket around her body tighter as a chill ran through her.

A dark figure stood behind the glass outside her front door.

She unlatched the safety bolt and prised the door open a little, feeling spooked by the sudden disturbance from a slumber.

"Come on Sandy, open the door!" Her sister Coral said, pushing on the door and feeling the resistance.

"Sorry... give me a..."

"Whoa the wind is mad out there." Coral said. Her face beamed bright red, Sandy noticed with guilt, as she opened the door and let her sister walk in to the hallway.

"You look frozen."

"Have you heard the news?" Coral asked, interrupting. Coral worked as a journalist at The Waterfell Way, the village's only newspaper. She'd dreamed growing up of ending up in London writing for one of the national broadsheets. But when their mum's health declined, she had remained at home to ease some burden for Sandy, two years her junior.

"What news?" Sandy asked, her mind still foggy. "Oh... Reginald's news?"

"How can you be so blasé?" Coral asked, pacing the living room. She moved like a ball of nervous energy. It was as if even her body was more in keeping with the London life she dreamed of than the sleepy village life she had ended up living.

"What else can I do?"

"Well... look, you don't like the man, but still..."

"Please don't tell me this might work out to be good for me."

"What?!" Coral asked, her face incredulous.

"I was asleep, I don't fancy doing this right now." Sandy said, taking a seat on her settee and pretending she was watching TV. The programme she'd been watching before falling asleep had finished. In its place was an antiques show where an elderly man was sending a rare book collection to auction.

"What on earth is wrong with you tonight?" Coral asked, standing in front of Sandy to block her view of the programme she didn't want to watch, anyhow.

"I want to mope a little. I know he's entitled to open his

own bookshop, but I also know it means I won't be able to compete with him."

"Compete with him?" Coral asked, stooping to Sandy's level. "Sandy, he's dead."

**

It turned out that Coral had hoped Sandy would know more than she did, so she could land an exclusive front page story.

All that Coral knew was that Reginald Halfman had died that evening, and that the police considered it to be suspicious. That announcement by Jim Slaughter had been made outside the Waterfell Tweed police station, and broadcast on every news station. Sandy had slept through the news broadcast.

"I didn't know about the shop." Coral repeated. "He actually announced it in your cafe?"

"He stood on one of my tables and called for attention from everyone. I wouldn't believe it myself if I hadn't been there."

The two sisters were sitting up in bed together, Coral borrowing a pair of Sandy's flannel pyjamas. Neither of them felt like being on their own.

"Who would do such a thing." Sandy muttered.

"He wasn't the most popular man." Coral said, which was true.

"And he didn't win me as a friend today but, still, I wouldn't wish the poor man dead."

"I bet it's a burglary." Coral said.

"You think?"

"Well, he's not quiet about how much money he's got, even if he lives - lived - in that dump. I think someone saw what valuables he had tucked away in there and he caught them."

"Hmm, I don't know. Surely if anyone would be targeted like that, it would be the Harlows." Sandy said. Benedict and Penelope Harlow lived in Waterfell Manor, the stately home set in 80 acres. Most of the village cottages had originally accommodated the Manor servants.

"I imagine they'll have a better security system than Reginald."

That was a good point. "You've got it all figured out."

"Well, it's what I do, isn't it... solve problems, like putting a jigsaw together without the picture on the lid?"

"Poor Reginald." Sandy said. She felt sick with guilt about her petty worries about her business. How could she have been so fixated on such trivial things? She remembered how just hours earlier she had even cursed Reginald's name as she had stood over a hot pan in her kitchen. As she had heated soup for dinner, he had been taking his last breaths.

"I don't think there's ever been a murder here." Coral said. "It will be big news. Extra newspapers need putting out, we'll have visitors coming to buy the Way and get the inside scoop.

"You never stop thinking about work, do you?" Sandy teased.

Coral laughed. "I'm still rehearsing for the nationals."

Sandy reached for her sister's hand and squeezed, then turned out the bedside lamp. She'd never told Coral, but she was pleased she hadn't left for the bright lights of the city. Coral may have given up a career, but by doing so, Sandy had gained a lifelong friendship with her sister.

Sandy couldn't imagine life without her sister by her side.

3

It was back to opening the shop alone before daylight the next morning for Sandy. Coral had left early so she could be the first one in the newspaper office as normal. Since then Sandy hadn't been able to shake off an uneasy feeling in the pit of her stomach.

She turned on all the lights in the shop and bolted the door behind her, then made sure she left the radio off. She wanted to hear if anyone tried to enter.

A single windowless envelope lay on the mat, addressed to 'Sandy Shore' in the unmistakable scrawl of Ignatius Potter.

Sandy's landlord was an eccentric hermit who had made her life difficult ever since she had taken on the business. His random letters would appear overnight instead of a personal visit.

They were always hand-scrawled and addressed to the wrong name, and told her off for things that weren't his business or suggesting ideas that were all ludicrous.

It was as if he imagined he was some silent partner and not just her landlord.

One letter had told her that selling cakes with nuts in would be the death of her business. Another advised that the first edition collection of Harry Potter books in the shop deserved a higher price tag.

She snatched the letter and moved into the kitchen.

She saw the kitchen and a wave of gratitude flooded her body that the kitchen was always thoroughly cleaned at night. It was dirty work, but she was always glad to arrive to clean work surfaces in the morning.

She placed the letter on the work surface and washed her hands. She was experimenting with a coconut and pistachio flapjack this morning and making the regular line up of cakes and cookies.

Sandy loved working with her hands, mixing ingredients, then celebrating the way they had rose or the glorious smell of a new combination. She got to see the success of her baking every day; twice - once as each cake was taken out of the oven and again when the customers savored them.

The morning went by fast as she focused on her work, and then her daily alarm went off to alert her to it being practically opening time. It had become daylight while she worked, the streets glistening from the rain that had fallen all morning. She unlocked the door and made herself a mocha, sitting with it in a seat that faced the door. She cupped the hot mug and had twenty glorious minutes of peace and quiet before the first face appeared at the door.

"Good morning." Dorie Slaughter greeted, looking left and right before heading straight for the table where Sandy was already sitting. "Have you heard the awful news?"

"About Reginald? Yes, Coral told me last night."

"Ah." Dorie said, sitting opposite her at the table. "My Jim was the first to know."

"Did he find him? Poor Jim." Sandy said, imagining how awful it must be to discover such a thing.

"No, he didn't find him. He got the call. First on the scene with the paramedics, but it was too late."

"It's so awful."

"Who'd even have access to poison, that's my question." Dorie pondered out loud.

"Poison? I thought it was a burglary gone wrong."

"Burglary? No!"

The door opened again and Cass walked in, her eyes red. She did just as Dorie had and joined the one table, grasping a hand of each of the two women already seated.

"What is the world coming to?" She asked, her voice breaking into a half-sob.

"Sandy considers it was a burglary," Dorie said before Sandy could object. She tried to avoid the village gossip mill as much as she could. "But burglars don't go armed with poison. It was planned, no accident."

"Well, he made no friends yesterday," Cass said.

"Cass!" Sandy exclaimed. Her friend always said precisely what she was feeling.

"I'm sorry Sandy, obviously I would wish no one dead."

"When were you going to tell me?" Sandy asked, regretting her words as soon as she had said them. She saw Dorie's ears perk up at the hint of tension and jumped up from her seat. "Let me get you drinks, ladies. The usual?"

She dived behind the counter and made their drinks, and by the time she returned, Penelope Harlow was hovering at the counter.

"Penelope, hello," Sandy called. She placed the drinks in front of Dorie and Cass and returned to the counter.

"Good morning, Sandy," Penelope replied. She was posh, all Hunter wellies and Ralph Lauren sweaters, but down to earth. Sandy liked her, not least because she presented the children's story time in the bookshop every Sunday morning.

"What can I get for you?" Sandy asked, deciding that she wouldn't be the first to mention the murder to customers. They might be visiting the cafe to escape the awful news.

"Two Americanos to go, please. Benedict's waiting out front."

Sandy looked through the shop window and saw Benedict sitting in the large Range Rover, a mobile phone pressed to his ear. He gestured with his hands as he spoke. Penelope followed her gaze, then looked at Sandy again and shrugged.

"The fundraiser was a huge success," Penelope said.

"Yes, everyone certainly threw themselves into it. I found out that you doubled the money raised?"

Penelope's cheeks flushed. The Harlows constantly supported the Waterfell Tweed community, with their time and their vast fortune, and they did so expecting no praise or recognition.

"Don't trust everything you discover," Penelope said with a small chuckle.

"I saw the figures in the newspaper." Sandy insisted. "I'm not trying to embarrass you, I wanted to say what a nice gesture it was."

Penelope shrugged. "I think that when you are blessed, you should build a longer table, not a higher wall."

Sandy nodded, realising the words summed up the Harlows.

"Well, lovely to see you, Sandy. This place is a little haven. Especially today." Penelope said and left with no further mention of the huge news.

"Can we talk?" Cass asked as soon as Penelope left. She

stood at the counter, her eyes still red. Dorie lingered in her seat, watching.

"Sure, come in the kitchen." Sandy said, wiping her hands on a tea towel by habit and leading Cass into the kitchen space.

Cass was a ball of nervous energy, picking at stumps of former talons. One finger began to bleed and Cass hastily placed her hand in her pocket.

"What did you mean, when was I going to tell you?" Cass asked.

"You know what I mean. When were you going to tell me you were letting your shop to Reginald Halfman so he could compete with me?!"

Cass blinked, open-mouthed.

"I know it's your business, Cass, and you don't have to tell me everything that's happening. But, hearing it from him was so humiliating." Sandy said. The whole thing sounded trivial aloud, especially given what had occurred in the interim.

"I don't know what you're talking about," Cass said.

"What?"

"I've hardly ever spoken to Reginald Halfman and my shop is busier than ever, why would I close?"

"But he told me. He came in here and announced it, yesterday."

"And I'm telling you it's not true," Cass said, her expression firm. "Don't you believe me?"

Sandy closed her eyes for a moment, imagining Reginald's showmanship the previous day and comparing it to her friend's quiet sincerity. "Of course I do. Of course, I believe you. Why would he have lied though?"

"Who knows? It's not worth worrying about now." Cass said.

"Reginald Halfman was well known for lying." A posh female voice called out from the counter behind them. Sandy turned to see Charlotte Harlow in her Burberry coat at the counter. Afforded a private education, she somehow lacked the down-to-earth personality that her parents had retained.

"What do you mean?" Sandy asked.

"There was no truth in his little show about him opening any kind of bookshop. I had my father check the council records and there's no mention of it at all. He was dreaming." Charlotte said, with a shrug. "I'll get a vanilla latte to go."

"Sure," Sandy said, busying herself with the intricate drink that Charlotte preferred.

"So it was all just a lie... how odd." Cass said. "What a strange man he was."

"He wasn't strange, he was horrible." Dorie Slaughter called from her seat. "He did some awful things and had no shortage of enemies."

"Dorie, please. He was eccentric that's all." Sandy said.

"Eccentric? Hmm. Ask Elaine about him." Dorie said, then sipped the last of her drink and stood up to leave.

Sandy watched the old woman leave the shop and brave the howling winds outside.

She certainly didn't have time to get involved in village gossip when a man lay dead.

4

*C*oral breezed into the shop five minutes after closing time, to Sandy's surprise.

"I'm in here!" she cried. She was sitting on the floor of the bookshop, making sure that the books were all in the right space. It was one of her favourite jobs. She turned the radio on to Classic FM and got to work, inspecting every single bookshelf to make sure everything was just so. It amused her to see how some browsers were utterly careless when it came to returning a book to a shelf; gardening books in the fiction section, true crime in the romance section, children's books with the cookery.

The bookshelves and their stock were her pride and joy. She had amassed them for years before opening the shop, filling a storage unit in the next village with stock she had bought from car boot sales and online auctions. And then a book owner friend rang her and offered her first refusal to buy the whole of his stock so he could retire. It had been her time - time to either turn the dream into a reality or give it up for good. She'd accepted his offer, rented the shop, and never regretted it for a moment.

"Are you mad?" Coral called, standing at the end of the bookshelf.

"Sitting down here? I love it." Sandy said. She was sitting with her legs crossed, something everyone commented on when they saw. A woman her age shouldn't be sitting cross-legged on a carpet, they thought. Sandy didn't care.

"No, leaving the door unlocked after closing when there's a murderer on the loose?" Coral cried. Her words sent a shiver down Sandy's spine. She hadn't considered that.

"Geeze, you're right." She jumped to her feet to lock the door, to find that Coral already had. There was a man's face looking in the door at her and Sandy jumped, until she recognised the face as being Jim Slaughter, the local constable. He gestured for her to open the door.

"Wow, it's freezing out there." He moaned as if the poor weather was a surprise. Waterfell Tweed had many selling points, its weather was not one of them.

"Are you here to speak to me about Reginald?" Sandy asked, only surprised that it had taken the officer so long to reach her on his rounds.

"What? No, no, unless you want to confess?" He asked, descending into a belly laugh. Jim was as round as he was tall, his hair thinning and he made even the police uniform look untidy. "I need a cake."

"A cake? We're closed, Jim." Sandy said. "And I thought you'd be busy with the murder investigation?"

"Me? Oh no, police from the city have been drafted in for that. DC Sullivan. He's a bundle of laughs... not." Jim said, eyeing up the cakes remaining on the counter. "Can I get a cake? You are still here, and every penny helps."

"What's it for?" Coral asked, standing behind Sandy.

"Well, I'm in a bit of trouble." Jim confided. "Today was mum and dad's wedding anniversary and I forgot. I need to get her something, make a bit of a fuss."

"That's good of you Jim. How many years would it have been?"

"Forty-five. It's been 28 without him, I barely remember him, but mum does. I think every year I need to put the date on my calendar and then forget."

"Ok," Sandy said, picking up her tea towel. "Here's what we'll do. Your mum's favourite is the coffee cake and I've got none left. If you can hang around for thirty minutes, I'll bake her a fresh one."

"You're a star, Sandy."

"There's one condition," Sandy said. "Get your calendar out now and write it in. Even a brilliant baker like me prefers a little notice."

"It's a deal," Jim said, a huge grin plastered on his face, revealing too many teeth in too small a space. "Thanks, Sandy."

**

"So what do you think of the news that city police are on the case?" Coral asked. The two sisters were sitting together in the cafe, each drinking a hot chocolate with cream and chocolate sauce.

"It's not a surprise, I guess. Jim's lovely but I can't imagine him catching a killer."

"They'll be dead formal," Coral said. "I see it when I cover the big stories. They close down, won't talk. Won't give quotes."

"But they'll solve the case, that's what matters?"

Coral shrugged. "I guess. Be nice to get an exclusive quote, though, and I could have done that with Jim."

"Maybe you still can." Sandy thought out loud. "Just because he's not working the case doesn't stop him having an opinion."

"Ooh, I like your thinking sis... very devious!"

Sandy rolled her eyes. Her sister was always plotting, always looking for the scoop, the next lead. Sandy was happy focusing on her next book to read.

**

Sandy had left her car at home that day. As she set off to walk home in the dark, she regretted that decision. She had never felt nervous walking around the village before, it was one of her favourite ways to relax and get a little exercise, but every shadow felt ominous and every noise made her jump. She was overcome with an overwhelming anger towards the person who had killed Reginald Halfman and shattered the peace and safety of the village she loved.

As she made her way down Church Street, she noticed a dark figure ahead and slowed her walking speed. She unzipped her handbag and pulled out her mobile phone, but it refused to turn on when she pressed the home button. "Damn." She cursed. No battery. She must remember to charge it more often.

As she put the phone back in her bag, she realised that the figure ahead had stopped walked and was standing, facing her. It looked like a man, and she could see in the half-light from a nearby lamppost that he was holding something long in his hand.

Before she even realised what she was doing, she turned and walked away. Footsteps behind her showed that she was being followed. She increased her speed, so did her assailant. She broke into a light run.

"Wait!" The voice called behind her, but she had no intentions of doing as he called. She looped back to the village square, let herself in the shop and locked the door behind her, then dived behind the counter. Her heart was racing. She set her phone to charge on the charger that was always left, but never used, next to the till. She would hide out in the shop until her phone was charged enough for her to ask Coral or Cass to come out and fetch her; they wouldn't mind.

After ten minutes, her heart rate had returned to normal. She was considering turning on a small light and making herself a mug of mocha, but was disturbed by a loud shout from outside. Peeking around the corner of the counter she saw, in the middle of the village square underneath a lamppost, her friend Cass. Sandy jumped to her feet, ready to call out and offer her friend help, but before she could reach the door, she saw another woman follow Cass.

"It was a mistake!" The woman called into the empty square. Sandy attempted to get a clear look at the woman but she was in darkness. All she could tell for sure was that it was a female voice.

"It's always a mistake. It was always a mistake." Cass said, her own voice quieter.

"He was a fool! But maybe we can be together now."

"I need time to think," Cass said. "It's gone so far now. I've lied because of you."

"I know, Cassie. I'm sorry."

Hearing the nickname sent a shiver down Sandy's spine. Nobody called her best friend Cassie. Who was this mysterious woman?

The woman turned and walked away. Cass dropped to the ground by the lamppost and covered her face with her hands. Sandy ached to run out and comfort her oldest friend, but couldn't give away her cover. Whatever she had just witnessed, she shouldn't have.

"Aargh!"

The loud cry made Sandy jump. The unknown woman had returned to the middle of the square, closer to Cass than she had been before.

"Just go," Cass said, and Sandy recognised that her friend was crying. "We can't be seen together."

The woman stepped into the light for a moment, opened Cass' hands and placed something into them, then turned and ran into the night.

Not wanting to attract any attention to herself, Sandy moved away from the cafe windows and settled herself on a beanbag in the children's section of the bookshop where she spent an unsettled night with little sleep.

**

The loud rapping on the door of the cafe roused Sandy out of her slumber. The bright sun shone in through the windows, hurting her eyes.

She wiped her eyes, walked into the staff toilet and gave her face a quick wash, sniffed at her armpits and straightened her ponytail, and heard yet more banging on the door.

"I'm coming," Sandy called, wondering how late she had slept.

An unknown man in a long coat, holding a tall umbrella in his hand, stood at the front door. Her assailant.

"Who is it?" She asked.

He reached into his pocket, and fearing the worst, Sandy stepped away.

"DC Sullivan, can you let me in? It's windy out here." He said, holding up his ID badge.

"DC Sullivan?" Sandy repeated, unbolting the door. The man was too young to work a murder case.

"Yes, that's me. Sandy Shaw, is that your real name?"

"Yes." She said, trying not to sound annoyed. The jokes about her and her sister's seaside names had stopped being amusing years ago.

"You're a hard woman to find."

"Really? I can't imagine I'm..."

"I posted a note through your door yesterday morning asking you to call the station, and then when I saw you last night, you turned and ran."

"So it was you last night? You unnerved me, a man in the dark following me."

The officer sighed. "Yes, I realised that. That's why I didn't chase you. You shouldn't be walking around on your own especially down deserted roads at nighttime."

"I realised it wasn't my best idea." Sandy realised the officer had been looking for, and must still want to speak to her. "Do you want a coffee?"

"Oh, no. I can't speak to you here. I'll need you to come down the station."

"Now?" Sandy asked, horrified.

"Later will be fine. It must be today. Come straight from work."

"Ok. Yes, I will. Are you sure I can't make you a drink to go, for your drive in?"

"I'm sure, thank you. Goodbye for now." DC Sullivan said, then turned and left the shop. Sandy grabbed her bag and left after him, locking the door behind her. She'd never opened the shop without having had a shower and wasn't about to start now, so she walked as fast as she could and let herself in her little cottage, bolting the door behind her. With the bathroom door bolted as well, she had the quickest shower she had ever had, being careful not to wet her hair. She was ready in record speed, dressed in her favourite pair of baggy jeans and an "I Love Waterfell Tweed" t-shirt that she had bought from the school two years ago as part of another fundraiser. She grabbed her rain mac and left the house, driving back to the shop. Her walking days were over, for now.

"What time do you call this?" Dorie asked, standing outside the door.

"Sorry, sorry!" Sandy apologised, unlocking the door. Dorie planted herself in her normal seat and picked up the menu which seemed unnecessary considering how long she had been a customer.

"Do you have any of those vegetarian sausages?" Dorie asked.

"What? Well, yes, I do... do you want one?"

"Ooh no. I'll get a full English today and a pot of tea."

"Coming right up," Sandy said, trying to hide her confusion.

Sandy disappeared into the kitchen and set the sausage, bacon, and egg to fry. As they cooked, she checked the cake supply from the day before. There should be enough. She was annoyed with how much the DC had unsettled her; all to tick her off his list of villagers he hadn't spoken to yet.

By the time she heard the bell of the door being opened and reappeared into the cafe, Elaine Peters had already sat down next to Dorie.

"Good morning, Elaine." Sandy said, pleased to see her

neighbour continue to get out and about. "What can I get you?"

"I'll have a veggie breakfast please, Sandy." Elaine said, her cheeks still flushed from the battering cold winds outside.

"Of course." Sandy said, hiding her surprise and returning to the kitchen. If Dorie, a fierce meat eater, had enquired about vegetarian sausages and Elaine was a vegetarian, this must be a planned meeting. Sandy hadn't thought the two had anything to do with each other.

She hung back near the counter and pretended to be checking tea bags.

"I can't believe I did that to him." Elaine whispered.

"It's for the best. I wish I'd been brave enough myself." Dorie said.

Sandy dropped the tub of tea bags on the floor where the ceramic pot had its fall broken by her big toe. "Ah!"

"Oh my, Sandy, are you ok?" Elaine called, up from her seat. She hovered on the other side of the counter, not one to enter a restricted space without permission.

"I'm so careless, sorry ladies. I'll be fine." She said and forced a smile. Dorie hadn't stood from her seat but was watching with curiosity.

Elaine gave a half-smile, nodded, and returned to the table where she and Dorie sat in silence until Sandy was out of earshot. Sandy tried to forget the conversation she had heard, and busied herself with preparing the two breakfasts.

When she returned out front, Dorie and Elaine were sitting on separate tables. Dorie smiled and accepted her breakfast as normal, but Elaine's eyes were red and puffy and she nodded at Sandy.

"Do you want a tea or coffee?" Sandy asked, realising that her customer hadn't ordered a drink.

Elaine shook her head, took a crisp £5 out of her purse and placed it on the table, and then pushed her chair back and left the cafe. When Sandy turned to Dorie, the older woman was concentrating on cutting her sausage.

Sandy picked up Elaine's plate, and her money, and returned behind the counter.

The bell rang again and in walked Cass.

"Hey, hun, can I get a cappuccino to go? My kettle's bust." Cass asked.

"Sure. How are you?"

"Oh, you know... same old."

"Do anything last night?" Sandy asked, attempting to sound nonchalant.

"Nah, just stayed in and watched rubbish on the TV." Cass said.

Sandy pictured her friend in the square, arguing with a mystery woman, and shook her head.

"You ok?"

"Yeah," Sandy said. "Just had a chill rush over me."

Cass left with the cappuccino and, for the first time since she'd known her, Sandy was pleased to see her leave.

"She's a strange one," Dorie called from her chair.

"We're all strange ones," Sandy said in reply. It was the peacekeeping thing she always tried to say, not wanting to involve herself in the village gossip, but she realised this morning that she really meant the words. She was learning increasingly, since Reginald Halfman died, that most of the villagers had a secret or two.

**

The rest of the day raced by, especially since Sandy ran out of cakes at 2 pm and had to apologise to everyone who came in afterward and offer them a savoury alternative. She could, if she'd had a staff member at work, have gone into the kitchen and made something from scratch, but with a killer on the loose, she didn't want to turn her back on the counter more than she had to.

One woman, a regular whose name Sandy had never known, opted for a caramel latte to get her sweet treat. Several others sat with only a drink while a couple even browsed around the bookshelves and bought new reading material when they couldn't buy a cake. Ordinarily, those latter people would have made Sandy delight, but she was too distracted by her upcoming meeting with DC Sullivan.

She'd been in the police station before and suspected most locals had. A village police station wasn't like what she imagined a city police station to be. It was a spoke in the community, just like every other business or organisation. Anyone doing a sponsored cake bake would traipse into the police station and cajole the officers to buy. Similarly, people would often wander in just for a chat, and parents would take their small children in to make them familiar with police so they didn't grow up scared of law enforcement, or to ask a police officer to tell them off for some minor wrongdoing.

Sandy didn't go in the station as often as some people did (Dorie Slaughter almost lived there when Jim was on duty - checking he wasn't too cold, checking what he wanted her to make him for dinner, telling him not to be late home). A few years earlier a child had gone missing, and the police had launched a huge manhunt; the child was found safe and well in a derelict shop hours after he should have returned home from school, and the police went down as quick-thinking heroes. Sandy couldn't help thinking that in her day, she was still playing or dawdling down by the river that long after school on many nights without the police being alerted, but she knew that times had changed. She had baked a Victoria sponge and walked it across to the station to present to the officers.

She locked the shop at 5 pm and walked across the village square and down High Street to the station and announced herself at the check in desk, where Jim Slaughter sat, reading a magazine.

"Busy?" She asked, indicating the magazine.

Jim shrugged. "Quieter than normal. They're keeping all the murder work to themselves."

"They?"

"Sullivan and his team."

"That must be frustrating," Sandy said. "I thought there'd be plenty of work to go around on such a big case."

"Nah, I'd be scared of doing something wrong, anyway. It's nice to have a bit of quiet time."

"Ah, Sandy Shaw, you made it." DC Sullivan called, appearing in the check-in area. "Follow me."

While Sandy had been in the station before, she'd never gone past the reception space. DC Sullivan led her into a tiny, uninteresting corridor with two doors off each side and two faded posters dotted along the wall. He opened the door to Room 3 and gestured for her to take a seat at the table.

"Drink?"

"Tea would be nice, please." She asked. He nodded and left the room, returning a few minutes later with two styrofoam cups of tea.

"So, if we can get down to it. I want to speak to you about Reginald Halfman, and your whereabouts on the night of his murder. I'm not cautioning you because you're not under suspicion, I'm speaking to you as a witness."

"Ok."

"Tell me how you knew Mr Halfman?"

"He was a regular customer in my shop; it's a cafe and bookshop. He would come in twice a week or so."

"Would you say you knew him well?"

"Not really. He was quite a character, so the things I knew about him were things he announced to the whole of the shop, not things he told me. He took out adverts in the newspaper, too, to announce things."

"What things?"

"Donations he had made, places he had been, that kind of thing."

"What did he do for work?"

Sandy frowned. "I have no idea,."

"That surprises you?"

"I never realised before. He had, erm, independent money."

"Like inheritance or money he had earned?"

"I couldn't tell you."

"Can you think of anyone who may have reason to want him dead?"

"No."

"Are you sure, Miss Shaw?" He asked, smirking at his play on her surname.

"Yes, I'm sure. He was an odd person, detective, and I can't say he won everyone over, but I can't imagine why anyone would want to kill him."

"Ok." DC Sullivan said. "And the last time you saw him?"

"The day he was killed. He came into my cafe, alone."

"And?"

Sandy took a deep breath. "He stood on one of my cafe tables and announced to everyone there that in a week's time he would open a shop right across the square, a cafe and bookshop that would be much better than mine."

DC Sullivan looked across at her. "How did that make you feel?"

"I was angry." Sandy admits.

"Surely anyone can start a business, even here in this little village. What did you have to be angry about?"

"I realised I didn't have any right to be angry... as soon as Reginald was killed, I realised that."

"Interesting choice of words." DC Sullivan said.

"What? Oh, I obviously didn't kill him, I meant it gave perspective. There I was upset with my friend and my business and a man was killed."

"Why a friend? You didn't describe Reginald as a friend earlier."

"No, not him. He owed me no loyalty. But the shop he was taking over was the shop of my friend, Cass Zuniper. I was upset that she hadn't told me first."

"I see. And where were you, on the evening that Reginald was killed?"

"I was at the shop, then I closed up, went for a walk, and then drove home. I live alone, and I fell asleep in front of the TV. My sister arrived as soon as she heard the news, and she stayed overnight with me."

"So nobody can corroborate your account until after the murder?"

"I guess not." Sandy admitted.

"Ok, thanks for your time, Miss Shaw."

5

*S*andy woke early the next morning after a fitful night's sleep.

She padded down the stairs in her slippers and into her kitchen, making herself a rich coffee to wake her up. She had asked Bernice to open the shop and make some of her most popular cakes to apologise to the customers who had gone without the day before. Bernice had been delighted to be asked and happy to help, leaving Sandy looking forward to a small lie in that she was frustrated hadn't materialised.

She took the coffee into her living room and sat in her reading chair, tucking her legs beneath her and pulling her dressing gown around her body. The house was always cold in the morning because she wasn't there long enough to make it worth putting the heating on for.

It was nice to have time to sit and enjoy a hot drink, something you don't get to do when it's your job to give other people those bursts of time for themselves.

Her mind kept returning to the interview the day before, how DC Sullivan had asked for corroboration for her account of where she had been. Sandy prided herself on being an honest person; she'd never thought or expected that her own word wouldn't be enough to be believed.

But then, the city police were used to dealing with people much less honest. They had to follow systems, not hunches. Everyone was a potential liar. A potential murderer. What a sad way to view the world.

Sandy decided that she would bake a cake for the police, to thank them for their hard work on the case. It couldn't be easy for them.

She jumped up and got herself dressed, pouring the rest of her coffee away and washing the cup.

She opened her door, grabbed her bag and screamed at the top of her lungs.

Lying face down on the path outside her house was her best friend, Cass.

**

The police arrived before the ambulance, and for a few moments, Sandy and DC Sullivan stood around Cass, not having enough medical knowledge to do anything other than look at her. Then the ambulance arrived, and the paramedics sprung into action.

"How old is she?"

"31."

"Any allergies, medical conditions?"

"No... not that I know of, no."

The paramedics, two men Sandy had never seen before, chatted with themselves then in shorthand that Sandy didn't understand. She watched the scene unfold as if it were happening to someone else, noticing that her body was shaking.

"You want to come with her?" One paramedic asked Sandy, who was about to say yes.

"No, she can't." DC Sullivan answered for her.

Sandy looked at him but said nothing.

"What happened to her?" Sandy asked.

The paramedics were placing Cass on a stretcher. She was lifeless, her beautiful hair bloodied.

"She's been hit with some kind of object. We'll know more at the hospital but I think she will be ok."

"She's alive?" Sandy asked, and the relief caused her sobs to come. She collapsed to the ground and allowed them to take over her body, crying for what could have been minutes or hours.

When she opened her eyes, DC Sullivan was standing over her.

"Sandy Shaw, I'm arresting you on suspicion of the murder of Reginald Halfman and the attempted murder of Cass Zuniper."

**

Sandy was returned to Room 3 where this time she was cautioned and the interview was recorded. Her whole body was still shaking with a delayed reaction to finding Cass.

"You cried when you were told Ms Zuniper was alive. You didn't cry when you thought she was dead. Why was that?"

"I don't know!" Sandy exclaimed. "I don't know the correct way to act in this kind of situation, and I'm sorry I got it wrong. I was just bottling things up and then when the paramedic said she was okay, I was so relieved. I couldn't hold it in anymore."

"You told me yesterday that you were upset with her."

"Yes, but I don't kill people I'm upset with!"

"Who do you kill?"

"Nobody!" Sandy cried. "This is ridiculous. You can't believe that I have done this."

"You have the motive to have killed Mr Halfman; he was going to open a competing business and, with your belief about his finances, he surely would have had the resources to be bigger and better - that was your fear, yes?"

"All of that is true except that it didn't make me kill him." Sandy said. "I'm a peacekeeper, I don't even argue with people never mind kill anyone."

"I see that a lot. People who bottle things in and then lose control and lash out. Is that what happened here?"

"No."

"I don't suppose you have anyone who can corroborate where you were this morning when someone was attempting to murder Cass Zuniper?"

"I live alone, DC Sullivan. There is nobody to corroborate my actions any morning."

"But usually you're in the cafe, baking cakes. The cakes themselves, if they're in the oven or freshly made, would effectively corroborate that that's where you were. Not this morning. Isn't that interesting?"

"I wanted a lie in. I asked a member of staff to open the shop."

"How convenient." DC Sullivan said.

"It's the -"

"It also suggests pre-meditation."

"What?"

"When did you arrange for this member of staff to do your morning duties?"

"Yesterday, I sent her a message and asked at around lunchtime."

"So we could say that you planned yesterday to do this today."

"No, it's not true."

The door opened then, and Jim Slaughter appeared in the doorway. He gave her a brief smile then turned his attention to DC Sullivan. "Can I have a word, guv?"

DC Sullivan stood up and approached Jim. They remained in the doorway, Jim whispering something to him. DC Sullivan sighed.

"Miss Shaw, I am told that a lawyer has arrived for you. Would you like to speak to them?"

Jim, standing behind DC Sullivan's back, gave a quick, urgent nod in her direction.

"Erm, yes, yes I would." She answered.

**

The lawyer was a woman. Ingrid Tate.

Sandy had seen her on local TV many times, being interviewed about various cases. She was dressed immaculately, her hair sprayed to within an inch of its life to maintain the beehive style it had been placed in.

"Ingrid Tate." The woman said, standing to shake Sandy's hand as she walked into the meeting room. Ingrid closed the door behind them. "So, Sandy, you're innocent right?"

"Of course."

"Forgive me, dear, I've never met you. I have to ask. Have you been answering questions?"

"Yes, of course."

"That's only a good idea if you really are innocent. Now you've been in there long enough, I will suggest you stop answering questions and leave the talking to me."

"Can I go home soon?"

"Sweetheart, if I wasn't here, you'd be going to prison, not home."

"What?"

"These police are lazy. They're out of their district to solve a crime they've got no interest in; nobody wants to be sent away from the exciting city to a little village like this, even for two murders. They want to find someone and get gone. You were nearly the scapegoat they want. Thank goodness I'm here."

"Who called you?"

"Hmm." Ingrid said. "That's the best part. It was Miss Cassandra Zuniper."

**

Less than an hour later, Sandy was back in her cottage.

Ingrid had told DC Sullivan that he had no evidence against Sandy at all, and when he sneered at that suggestion, Ingrid had quoted pieces of law to him, until he had agreed to allow Sandy to go - for now.

She went into the bedroom and changed out of her clothes into the fleecy pyjamas she loved, then pulled her dressing gown on. She was chilled to the bone.

A quick glance at her phone showed a message from Bernice asking if everything was OK and saying that she had remained in the shop all day. It made Sandy grateful that she had a friend who was so unflappable.

It was 6.30pm, and Sandy collapsed onto her bed but found she couldn't sleep.

Reginald Halfman's murder had unsettled her, but an attack on her best friend? And if the police were as lazy as

Ingrid Tate suggested, ready to lock up the first person they could for the crimes, then maybe Sandy needed to take matters into her own hands.

For her friends' safety.

And to prove her innocence.

6

*A*fter a fitful night's sleep, Sandy was in the shop's kitchen earlier than normal, whipping up batches of her most popular cakes, which she planned to offer for a special one-day-only low price.

If she wanted to solve the crimes, her first step had to be information gathering - and her very own cafe was the best place to do that.

Before the shop opened, she had a Victoria sponge, a lemon drizzle cake, a fruit loaf, chocolate chip cookies and a coconut tart all ready and displayed.

She waited for a few minutes while her ancient printer fought to produce an A4 sign for the door.

"Happy World Kindness Day - Cake Sale today only!"

She hadn't even finished blu-tacking the sign when the first customer came in.

"Are you ok?" Bernice Alton asked, her eyes wide. She grabbed hold of Sandy and pulled her in for a hug.

"I'm ok, Bernice, I promise," Sandy said. Bernice must have heard on the gossip grapevine about her being arrested. "Does everyone know?"

"Cass rang me from hospital. An officer had gone to see her and told her - as if the case was closed! - that they'd arrested you. She rang and told me everything, and I told her you needed a lawyer. She sorted the rest. I think everyone else will think you were giving a statement."

"Thank you," Sandy said, believing Bernice's words. Bernice was one of the few people in the village who didn't get involved in gossip. That was probably why Cass had chosen her to phone. "How is Cass?"

"She will be fine. She should be home in a couple of days. People can visit... but, I don't know if..."

"I'll be going after work. DC Sullivan won't stop me going to visit my best friend."

Bernice broke into a smile. "Good girl."

"Bernice, what do you think about Reginald Halfman's murder? Who could do such a thing? Do you think the same person attacked Cass?"

"I don't think it's the same person," Bernice said. "Whoever killed Reginald made sure the job was done. Cass was hit, with an object, once. I can't help wondering if someone with a grudge against Cass decided now was the time to hurt her, and make it look connected to the murder."

Sandy's stomach flipped at her friend's words. "Oh my God... so there could be two attackers out there?"

"Do you know anyone who would want to hurt Cass?" Bernice asked. "You know her better than anyone."

"No. There's nobody." Sandy said, shaking her head. But her mind returned to the scene in the village square a few nights before, Cass arguing with a mysterious woman. Maybe she didn't know Cass that well.

She returned to the counter and grabbed her trusty diary, flicking back a few pages to the date in question. She stood and scribbled everything she could remember about the argument, including the time and as much as she could think of to describe the woman. Then she turned to the page for the day before and wrote about Cass being attacked. Could it be a coincidence?

"I'm going to stick around today." Bernice said. "And don't try to talk me out of it. Don't pay me if you can't, but you need support right now."

Sandy smiled at her. "Thank you, Bernice. That means a lot."

The bell rang, announcing a visitor, and in walked the Harlow family. Benedict and Penelope sat down at a table, while their daughter Charlotte wandered into the bookstore part of the shop.

"Good morning," Benedict called out. "We are here to show our support."

"Thank you, Benedict. Penelope." Sandy said, walking over with a notepad to take their order. She'd never mastered the art of memorising orders. She appreciated them being there. They were the faces of Waterfell Tweed, and their faces being in her cafe would be great for business, and her reputation.

"Such an awful business," Penelope said, reaching for Sandy's hand. "How is Cass?"

"She will be ok. Actually, I'm going to visit her later."

"Pass on our regards, please?" Benedict asked. The two of them looked fresh from a countryside magazine; him with his tweed jacket and her with her Hunter wellies and raincoat.

"Of course. What can I get for you?"

"I'll have a black coffee," Penelope said.

"Tea please, and get us a couple of those scones."

"And for Charlotte?"

"Oh - I quite forgot she was here!" Penelope admitted

with a laugh. "Let her order for herself when she's finished browsing. Who knows how long she will be when there are books around."

"What's she doing back? She seems to be home more often than normal." Sandy asked.

Benedict leaned into her. "I don't think she's thrilled in the city."

"Oh no, that's a shame," Sandy said, unsure of what else to add. She'd never felt a connection with Charlotte Harlow, despite them being similar ages.

She retreated from the table and got on with making the drinks, under Bernice's watchful eye.

"Bernice, I'm ok." She said.

"Hmm." Her friend replied.

Charlotte Harlow didn't emerge from the books until her parents had finished their drinks. Sandy would usually be excited to have such a keen book lover in the shop, but in her experience, Charlotte was a browser, not a buyer. True to form, she reemerged, empty-handed.

"Americano, please Sandy." She called across, even though Sandy was at another table taking an order from a stranger who was out hiking in the area. Sandy gave a thumbs up to acknowledge the order.

The hiker was a nervous-looking man, wrapped up in more clothes than was necessary for the weather, all of which he kept on his body despite being indoors. Sandy took his order as fast as she could and then asked Bernice to prepare the complicated order, which was a breakfast from the menu with every item replaced or changed.

She made Charlotte's coffee and returned to their table.

"No books take your fancy?" She asked. Browsers didn't pay the bills.

Charlotte furrowed her brow. "Oh plenty, I took a photo of the covers. I prefer to read on my phone."

"Ah." Sandy said as Charlotte held up her enormous phone. It must be the latest model, only released a few days ago. Charlotte Harlow wouldn't have queued overnight for it, as a few of the younger villagers had; she probably had a member of staff to do things like that for her.

"You'll be relieved there's no competitor opening, I imagine," Charlotte said.

"I'd rather a competitor than a man dead," Sandy said, and the words were true. Despite her initial anger at Reginald's business idea, she had come to realise that a second bookshop, and a third and a fourth, would be good for her business. They'd give Waterfell Tweed the reputation of being a book town, like Hay-on-Wye in Wales, and attract book lovers. If only she'd had a few days to get her head around the surprise, it could have been exciting for her and Reginald.

"He'd have been awful in the book business," Charlotte said.

"Charlotte," Penelope warned.

"It's true, mummy. He had no respect for the written word. At least you -" Charlotte said, then paused. The tone of her voice as she addressed Sandy appeared to be harsher than she meant. "You, Sandy, you love books. Like I do."

"But you don't read them," Sandy said.

Charlotte laughed. "Oh, I would, if my life was different. A city life leaves no room for books. If I was living here, like you, my house would overflow with the things."

"You don't have to stay there forever, darling," Benedict said to his daughter, who rolled her eyes.

"Can we talk about something else? This is frightfully

dull." Charlotte said, picking up her cup to take a sip of her drink.

Sandy smiled at the three of them and then returned to the counter.

The door opened again and in walked her sister, Coral.

"Hey, sis." She said. "Can I get a porridge and a mug of tea?"

"Sure, I'll bring it over," Sandy said.

Coral turned and saw that there were several empty tables. "It's ok, I'll stand and chat. Have you heard the news?"

"What news?"

"About Cass? She was attacked." Coral said.

"Oh, yes, I know that news. That was yesterday, sis, you're a bit out of date."

Coral laughed. "They sent me to Manchester yesterday on a course, and get this - no signal. No signal on the train, thanks for nothing Richard Branson, and no signal in the building."

"Wow. How did you cope?"

"I'm going to get compensation. How can people live like that? Even here we get a good phone and WiFi signal. It's so... 18th century!"

"18th century? I don't think the biggest concern then was good WiFi."

"Well, it's my biggest concern now. I kept turning my phone on and off to test it, I couldn't believe a place would have no WiFi... its... anyway, how is she?"

"I'm going to visit her later." Sandy said. "I can't believe you've only just found out."

"Why would I find out earlier, sis? What happens here is no news at all in the city."

Sandy frowned. Something about her sister's words

caused her to stop. Gave her a thought she couldn't quite reach. Unlocked a memory, or a premonition.

Coral had disappeared to secure a table, and no sooner had she left the counter than the door opened again, and in walked Gus Sanders, the man who ran the butcher's on the square. He was a rare visitor in the shop.

"Good morning Gus, how are you?"

"Better now I've seen that there's a cake sale!" He said, laughing. "I'll take three slices of lemon drizzle please for me and the lads."

"Is that to go?"

"Yes please... see if they last until lunchtime!" He said, with another laugh.

Sandy took the lid off the cake dome and found one of her sharpest knives.

"How have you been, Gus? Any news?"

"Only the graffiti on the shop again. I've told the police but they've got better things to do right now... awful business isn't it?"

"It really is." Sandy said. "I didn't know the graffiti was still happening."

"It stops and starts. Annoying, but I guess people have bigger problems."

Gus had first been targeted by a graffiti artist a few months earlier, when an abusive message calling him an animal killer had been sprayed on the front of his shop. Since then, the spray painting incidents had been sporadic, and always targeted at his shop only.

"Well, if I hear of any angry vegans, I'll be the first to let you know." Sandy joked.

Gus raised a weak smile. "Tell the police, not me, or I might be called in for questioning myself."

He took his bags of cakes and left the shop, waving his

goodbye. His words caused Sandy's cheeks to flush. He was the first to mention her police experience in such a light-hearted way, and while Sandy trusted that his intentions were good, she still found herself unsettled.

She looked across the counter into the kitchen to see Bernice watching her with concern.

7

*I*t was rare that Sandy ever took a lunch break, but after Gus Sanders' words, she struggled to stop her hands shaking and felt close to tears. She told Bernice that she was going to go for a walk to clear her head, and Bernice nodded her agreement.

Sandy pulled on her bright yellow rain mac and made herself a mocha to go, then set out on foot. It was a crisp autumn day, and the leaves crunched underneath her boots as she stomped her way across the village square. She followed the roads to the church and settled herself on a wooden bench underneath a large oak tree. It was serene and quiet, and a squirrel ran out in front of her, making her smile for the first genuine time since she had found Cass lying outside her door.

Sandy took out her notebook and looked at the page she had written the day before. She must have been beyond exhausted when she attempted to get her thoughts out because she couldn't read a single word of her notes. She looked at the indecipherable scribble and let out a small laugh.

"Well, things happen for a reason." She muttered under her breath and turned to a fresh page.

She wrote in large letters REGINALD on one side of the paper, then CASS on the other side, and enclosed each name in a circle.

Immediately, she realised that the only thing that connected them both was Cass' business premises; the premises that Reginald said he would take over, and which Cass insisted she was remaining in. Surely that spurious link gave nobody motive to hurt them both unless it was a person who was also keen to have the premises for themselves. But that was hard to imagine. There weren't that many people in the small village who wanted to begin a business; most were traditional folk employed in careers that they had had for decades.

She wrote next to Cass' name, 'argument' and 'who is the mystery woman', but had little to write next to Reginald's name.

All she could add was 'poison', but she had no idea who might have access to a poison. The village pharmacy had closed the year before, leaving the villagers having to trek into the next town for their medication needs.

There had been, and still was, huge uproar about this. Soon, a new pharmacy would be built attached to the doctor's surgery, but the building hadn't even begun yet.

She sighed and put the lid back on her pen. It appeared she was hardly cut out for detective work.

Sandy remembered the look that DS Sullivan had given her, how certain he appeared that he had found the murderer, and a chill went up her spine. She needed more information, and she knew where to go.

**

Jim Slaughter was precisely where Sandy expected him to be, sitting in his car eating a hot dog from the mobile van that turned up every week and parked up in the field that hosted the car boot. He'd shared often how the sausage and fried onion lunch was his treat whenever he wasn't on duty, and when Sandy had poked her head in the station and discovered that he was off, she knew where to find him.

"Hello Jim, can I have a word?" She asked, letting herself into his passenger side. Her interruption made him jump and a splodge of mustard landed on his faded jeans.

"Blimey, Sandy... what are you doing here?"

"I was looking for you."

"Oh..." Jim said, covering his hot dog with a napkin.

"Keep eating, please. I don't want to disturb you, I needed to speak to you - alone."

Jim gazed at her, a bead of sweat appearing on his lip.

"You obviously know DC Sullivan arrested me yesterday."

Jim coughed. "Yes... yes. I'm glad you accepted the lawyer."

"I need your help, Jim, or that city cop will frame me for murder!"

"How can I help you? I'm stuck on reviewing Freedom of Information requests, I probably know less about the case than you do." He said, exasperated. Sandy felt sorry for him; imagine being cut out of your first murder case.

"I don't understand why DC Sullivan doesn't recognise what you could offer to the case. With your local knowledge, you must have so many ideas he's never thought of."

"Well, I have a few."

"I bet you do. I mean, I bet you have an idea why

someone would want Reginald and Cass dead?" Sandy asked, hoping she had flattered Jim enough to drop his guard.

"Well, that's just it. That's exactly what DC Sullivan's missing."

"What is?" Sandy asked. Jim eyed her warily. "Please, Jim..."

"They didn't want Cass dead, Sandy. It was you they were after."

**

After the shock of Jim's words, the idea made perfect sense.

Who would have expected Cass to be at Sandy's house early in the morning?

The two of them looked similar, both had long brown hair and such a similar build that they shared clothes sometimes. From the front, they were different; Cass' heavy make-up was visible from afar while Sandy preferred the more natural look. But from behind? Anyone would have thought it had been Sandy, perhaps locking her front door, and not Cass, perhaps just about to knock.

The realisation sent a chill down Sandy's spine.

"Are you ok?" Jim asked. "I could be wrong, I mean I'm not smart enough to be giving my opinion at work, or being asked for it, so don't let it worry you."

"No, no... it makes perfect sense. It's so obvious now, I can't believe I didn't think of it. I can't believe DC Sullivan hasn't thought of it! The man's a fool, Jim."

"He just thinks city knows best," Jim said with a resigned shrug. The napkin coated hot dog sat in his lap.

"Come on, I'm going to buy you the biggest hot dog they sell," Sandy said, leading the way out of the car. Jim followed without a word of objection. "It's the least I can do."

The car boot was finishing now, most of the sellers had packed up their remaining odds and ends and left. Only a few stragglers remained, trying to convince the hardy sellers to reduce prices further.

"I never understand car boots myself." Jim said, looking out at the scene while Sandy ordered his hot dog.

"Why's that?"

"I've got enough junk at home, I don't need to buy other people's."

"Ooh I don't know, I quite like the adventure of it. You never know what you might find. Not everything is as it appears to be, PC Slaughter, you should know that better than most."

He gave a toothy grin and took a huge bite out of the sausage, dropping a dollop of ketchup on to his left trainer. He didn't appear to notice.

"Well, I'll be off. Thanks for your help, Jim." Sandy said.

"Shall I give you a lift?"

"No, you stay and enjoy your lunch." She said, trying to ignore the uneasy feeling in her stomach at the thought of walking back to the cafe alone. It was broad daylight, and only a five-minute walk, but she felt very aware that she was alone, and potentially unsafe. She quickened her pace and tried to listen out for noises over the sound of her drumming heartbeat.

As soon as she saw the cafe come into view, she felt more relaxed but didn't slow her pace. By the time she reached the front door, she burst in with more force than she planned, causing the few customers to all look at her. Meanwhile, Bernice pursed her lips with concern.

"Are you ok?" Bernice asked.

"I'm fine." Sandy said. "More unfit than I realised!"

"Sit down, let me get you a drink."

"I'm fine, honestly, I'd rather keep busy." Sandy insisted, replacing her coat with the apron she always wore in the shop. She walked into the small kitchen and washed her hands even more thoroughly than normal, giving her time to control her breathing. "Right, that's better."

As Sandy walked out from the kitchen into her familiar cafe, she couldn't help looking at each face in turn and wondering whether that person had tried to hurt her. It was an unsettling feeling after years of feeling certain that she knew who her friends were.

"Looks like you've seen a ghost, Sandy." Dorie Slaughter called, sitting in her regular seat with a jacket potato and salad on a plate in front of her.

"Oh you know, Dorie, just a long day." Sandy said, deciding to sit down with the elderly customer for a few minutes. Bernice was more than capable of managing things. "How are you doing?"

"Not well, I have to say," Dorie admitted. "All this business, it's playing heck with my irritable bowel. Look what I'm having to eat now, I'd much rather a slice of that fruit cake!"

"It doesn't look that appetising, does it?" Sandy admitted, looking at the plain jacket potato. It would be a lovely lunch with a dollop of butter and some grated cheese, but on its own it didn't spark much excitement in her.

"I don't trust that DC Sullivan to solve these crimes." Dorie said, her face genuine, as if her opinion was unbiased.

"They've come in and pushed my Jim out, and he's worth ten of them!"

"I don't disagree." Sandy muttered.

"Was it awful, love?" Dorie asked, leaning in close.

Sandy nodded, feeling embarrassed as her eyes filled with tears. She took a deep breath and forced a smile on her face. "I'll be fine, Dorie, don't worry about me."

"The next victim could be any of us, Sandy, and DC Sullivan's focusing on the wrong woman."

"The wrong woman?" Sandy asked.

"Well, it must be a woman."

"What makes you say that?"

"I shouldn't tell you this." Dorie said, leaning in even further. Her breath smelt of the red onion from her salad. "But the footprints are from a female's shoe."

"What footprints?"

"Footprints at Reginald's house. You won't believe this, but his carpet was brand new that day. One of those really thick, heavy piled ones. You know that carpets need to breathe? Don't walk on them for 12 hours or so, that's what they say when you buy a really nice one. Well, the murderer wouldn't have known it was new. And when the police got there, there were footprints on the carpet. Only a few, she obviously realised she was leaving a mark and whipped her shoes off."

"How do they know it's a woman's shoe, though?" Sandy asked.

"Stilettos, Sandy. And I've never seen you wear stilettos in all the time I've known you."

Sandy took out her notebook and stood up, excusing herself from the table. She stood right at the back of the small kitchen and turned to the page she was writing on earlier, adding "KILLER IS A WOMAN - STILETTO SHOES" to Reginald's page.

"Are you sure you're ok?" Bernice asked, entering the kitchen.

Sandy stole a quick glance at her ballet pumps, then met her gaze.

8

*R*eginald's funeral took place on a bitter cold day, that day that occurs each year where autumn feels much more like winter. Sandy sent a wreath but couldn't join most of the villagers in attending the service, as she was preparing the food for the wake.

While most other people walked to the church, she locked the shop, because she had an uneasy feeling about being alone in the kitchen where she couldn't see who was coming in. Sandy hated feeling scared in her own beloved shop, and the feeling made her more determined to catch the real killer.T

The radio was tuned to Classic FM while she busied herself preparing a sandwich platter, mini pork pies and quiches, a beautiful fresh salad, and a tray of sliced melon. Next she turned her attention to making a large Victoria sponge, the cake that would please the most people in any crowd. She filled it with extra jam and cream and topped it with fresh sliced strawberries, then stood back to look at the food.

Sandy hoped it would be enough, as she always did

when she made a buffet. It always looked as though the food couldn't feed the number of people it was for, and then there were always leftovers. It was like magic.

Satisfied with the food, she washed her hands and patted them dry on the tea towel, then unlocked the front door and opened the boot of her car. It took four separate runs to fill her car with the buffet food, the cold air hitting her each time she left the warmth of the shop.

The drive to The Tweed public house was walkable, it was just a few doors away, but Sandy hadn't fancied carrying the platters one at a time. As she opened her car door, the heavens opened and a heavy downfall started. Determined not to look like a drowned rat when the mourners arrived, she shut the door again and sat in the car, watching the droplets of water hammer down on her windscreen.

After a few moments, a slight figure in a dark dress ran by the side of the car and into The Tweed, and then the rain stopped with as little warning as it had started.

Sandy began the trips into the pub, balancing a platter in her arms.

Tom Nelson, the landlord, rushed out from behind the bar when he saw her.

"Come, Sandy, let me grab that."

"Thanks." She said, accepting his offer. She returned to the car for another platter, and with Tom's help, they made quick work of moving all of the platters and the cake box to the pub. The wake would take over the whole of the pub, as every one of the local funerals did. It was inconceivable that anyone local would go in the pub for anything but a wake, when one was happening, and any tourists or out-of-towners had to take second place to raising a glass for the departed.

"Need a hand setting it up?" A woman asked, as Sandy arranged napkins and paper plates.

She turned to see the woman who had ran into the pub a few minutes before. It was Elaine Peters, and she looked beautiful. Her face was transformed by subtle make-up and the plain black dress she was wearing hugged her body in all the right places. Elaine had a wobbly tummy, by her own confession, but somehow the lines of the dress she was in drew attention to her cleavage and her shapely legs.

"You look gorgeous, Elaine!" Sandy said, then wondered if that was an inappropriate thing to say at a wake. Her eyes glanced down, and spotted the stiletto shoes that Elaine was wearing. The sight of them reminded Sandy of Elaine's conversation with Dorie just days earlier, about the man who had had it coming to him. Could Elaine by the person who had tried to kill her?

"Oh, stop." Elaine said, blushing. "I thought I'd make a bit of effort."

"Are the others on their way?" Sandy asked, looking around the empty pub.

"No, not yet." Elaine said. "I couldn't handle it, I had to get away. It... it brought back too many memories."

Sandy nodded. Elaine had appeared to have made such progress, getting out and enjoying life again after being widowed, and then the murder happened.

"Everyone will understand," Sandy said. "Was it a good turnout?"

"Yes," Elaine said, "Probably better than he deserved. Oh, I shouldn't say that, but he was no friend of mine. After Martin died, he tried to push me into selling my cottage."

"Really? I never knew."

"I told no one, I was so ashamed. It was right after Martin died, and Reginald turned up at my front door pretending to be concerned about me, and whether I could afford my mortgage. Said he would offer me a good deal if I needed a quick sale so I could downsize. Downsize?! Ha!"

The thought of Elaine being able to downsize from her small cottage was entertaining, but despite its size, it was easy to imagine why Reginald would have wanted to own it. It was a beautiful old building, and Elaine and her late husband had done plenty to keep the original features. The cottage still boasted a thatched roof, the original wooden beams inside, and sash windows.

"What did you say?"

"I told him I'd think about it. I was too stunned to say anything else and, to be honest, I was clueless about money back then. It turned out that the life insurance paid the mortgage off, but I didn't even know it existed then. And, if that was as much as Reginald had done, maybe I'd think he was acting out of concern. But he wouldn't let it drop, even after I told him I didn't need his help. He kept turning up at the cottage, he'd stand across the road and watch me. It was very... unsettling."

"You should have told me, Elaine. I could have helped."

"I wasn't really seeing or telling anyone anything then, Sandy, don't take it personally. It was an awful, awful time, and that horrible man made it harder than it had to be."

Sandy reached over and gave Elaine's hands a squeeze as the pub door burst open. In walked the Harlow family, Charlotte leading the way. She strode in, her high heels clicking across the tiles of the floor, followed by her parents. Penelope was also in heels, and Sandy realised that checking footwear today would be pointless. Everyone was dressed in their finest clothes and fanciest shoes.

"What a waste of a morning." Charlotte hissed, standing at the bar. She hadn't noticed Sandy and Elaine who were off to the side, in the shadows as they arranged the food over a long decorating table that had been erected especially for the occasion.

"Oh, Charlotte, enough." Penelope chided.

"I don't know why you made me go."

"We have to be seen." Benedict explained. "We play an important role in this village, our family name matters. You need to realise that if you're going to move back."

The mention of Charlotte returning to Waterfell Tweed for good made Sandy pay attention, but the conversation went no further. Benedict ordered a shandy for himself and a glass of white wine each for his wife and daughter, and they sipped in silence at the bar until the door opened again and the mourners piled in. They must have walked back, the Harlows would have driven.

Sandy stood back, slipping into catering mode. When she was working on a corporate gig, which she did rarely, she tried to become invisible.

Reginald had no family attend the funeral apart from a tall uncle, who left the wake within half an hour. He seemed to have drawn the short straw and attended as the family representative out of duty rather than any genuine grief. The atmosphere was strange after that, with no official mourners to pass the obligatory "I'm sorry for your loss" wishes on to, it felt less like a wake and more like a village get together.

The food went down well, and the drink did too. Gus Sanders seemed the most jovial, ordering shots at the bar for anyone who would join him, while his wife Poppy sat alone with a tonic water.

"Are you ok?" Sandy asked her, offering her a sandwich from a platter.

"Oh, I'm fine... it's him who isn't." Poppy said. "Making a

bloody fool of himself and he'll be expecting me to carry him home later."

Sandy was about to reply when she realised that Poppy was smiling. Her comment was good-natured.

"1-2-3 DOWN IN ONE!" Gus cried from the bar to a round of applause. Sandy smiled at Poppy and moved on, offering the remaining sandwiches around the group.

"Come on Jim, help a girl out and have another sandwich." She said, finding Jim Slaughter sitting at a table with Elaine Peters. He blushed at the sight of Sandy, but reached out to the platter and took another three sandwiches. To Sandy's surprise, he put two on Elaine's plate, and one on his own.

Sandy raised an eyebrow and moved on.

Penelope and Charlotte Harlow were deep in conversation when she reached their table. Benedict was at the bar, always one of the men when he had the chance.

"Ladies, help me out and have another sandwich?"

"Not for me, dear, but thank you ever so much." Penelope said, smiling.

"Charlotte?" Sandy said.

"No." Charlotte replied. The bluntness of her refusal made Sandy jump, but she said nothing and left them to it.

Finally she reached the table where Coral and Cass were sitting, and took a seat with them.

"Bit strange, isn't it?" Cass asked, her big eyes wide and searching.

"Wakes always are." Sandy said with a shrug.

"It's more than that, sis. It's like everyone in here is celebrating not mourning. Reginald Halfman upset a lot of people." Coral said, nursing a glass of red wine in her hand.

"I need to tell you something." Sandy said. They both

moved in closer to her. "I don't think anyone meant to hurt you, Cass."

"Well, they did a good job!" Cass said, reaching to the spot on her head where she had been hit. The area protruded like an egg growing out of the side of her head.

"No, they got the wrong person."

"But who did they think I was?" Cass asked, while Coral's hand shot to cover her mouth.

"They thought it was you." Coral said, her whole face and neck growing red with fury. "We need to tell the police."

"There's no point." Sandy said. "The city police just want to find the easy target and close the case. They're going to charge me unless I can find out who the real killer is and prove it."

"But who would want to hurt you Sandy? Reginald upset a lot of people, but you haven't got enemies like he had."

"Well, I've got at least one enemy. The key is working out who it is."

"There must be something linking you and Reginald." Coral said, her investigative mind clicking into gear. "Something that would make a person want you both out of the way."

"What on earth could link me and him? I know! I think I've got it!" Sandy called, causing other people to look around. "Come on, let's get out of here. We'll go to my place, it's more private."

The three of them stood and climbed into Sandy's car, driving the short distance to her house, where she made them each a big mug of steaming hot coffee before they settled down on her two plush leather settees.

"So, you think you've got an idea?" Coral asked, a doubting eyebrow raised.

"Yes, I think so. It's books."

"Books?" Cass asked.

"I have the bookshop, Reginald announced opening a bookshop. It has to be the link."

"Nobody would kill people because they like books, Sandy. He was hardly suggesting he was planning on opening, ooh, a strip club!" Coral said with a laugh.

"It has to be the link. It has to be." Sandy said, although her belief was dimmed by the response of the two people closest to her. Coral and Cass began to chat about other subjects, and Sandy wondered if she was out of her depth attempting to solve the case.

9

*S*andy woke early and went straight to the shop.

It was another cold day, and the drizzle had fallen nonstop since the evening before when she had said goodbye to Coral and Cass after a disappointing evening of discussing everything apart from the case.

After her suggestion that herself and Reginald were connected by a common interest in books, Sandy had felt foolish and offered little more to the conversation. After an hour or gossiping about common friends and enemies, her best friend and sister seemed to realise that Sandy was even quieter than normal and suggested they leave. Sandy hadn't argued. She'd shown them out into the drizzle, giving a half-hearted offer to drive them both home, and had felt relief when they'd refused.

After she'd bolted the door behind them, she had slumped down to the ground and cried. There were few things Sandy hated more than feeling she had embarrassed herself; it was why she kept a low profile in most conversations. Plenty of people opened their mouths too often and proved themselves to be fools; at least silence could give the pretence of wisdom.

After another fitful night's sleep, Sandy had seen the alarm clock flick from an hour that began with a four, to one beginning with a five, and had given up the attempt for further rest. She'd had a long, scalding hot bath and allowed her skin to dry as she lay on her bed wrapped in a towel. Then she dressed in her most comfortable pair of jeans and a thick jumper and drove to the shop.

When she opened the shop, the cafe was an afterthought. Her dream had been the bookstore, a treasure trove crammed to the rafters with new and second-hand books, a sanctuary where everyone would find something they liked. She had spent years finding and stashing away book collections, waiting for the right time to move ahead with her dream. When the property came on the rental market, she had had a look around, ignoring the obvious space for some kind of food outlet and picturing instead bookcase after bookcase.

But then she considered her own book-buying habits; the way she gravitated towards the smell of a coffee as much as the range of books on offer, how she returned to one sweet little bookshop not only because of its books but because of the lemon cake for sale in its cafe.

Coffee, and books.

Cakes, and reading.

The two seemed to go hand in hand.

Books and Bakes had been born.

And it turned out that the people of Waterfell Tweed enjoyed the bakes so much, the cafe grew and grew, forcing Sandy's beloved books to take over just under a third of the ground floor space.

Convinced that her investigative skills weren't what they

needed to be, Sandy had thrown her heart back where it belonged: her beloved shop.

She unlocked the door and flicked on the lights, appreciating the clean and tidy way it looked in a morning. Cleaning up at the end of a long day was everyone's least favourite job, but she was always so pleased it had been done when she arrived again to open the shop. She locked the door behind her and hung up her yellow mac, placing her handbag behind the cafe counter and turning on the radio.

Then, she turned around to face her bookshop in all its glory.

A dream she never really believed could come true, right in front of her. She allowed herself a smile.

"Good morning, books." Sandy whispered, then laughed at her own silliness. While she knew a book wouldn't answer her, at times, books had been her closest friends and greatest teachers.

Next, she inspected every single book, pulling each one off the shelf and giving it a wipe with a dry cloth if needed. She checked the sticker price on every book, and the few she found without stickers she wrote a price out there and then. These were the jobs she imagined would fill her days before she opened, instead of making drinks and washing pots. She pulled out books about trains from the travel section and books about animals from the trains section.

As she made progress through the bookshelves, the tightness in her shoulders eased and the swirling feeling in her stomach disappeared.

The books were her sanctuary. Just as they'd always been.

A loud rapping at the door startled her, causing her to

drop the book she was just filing back into place onto her foot. She stood up, realising that she needed to push up with a hand to get her frame from the floor and wondering when that change had occurred. She was too young to notice her body changing in these ways, she felt sure. Only in her early 30s and yet already her body had sagged in places and she was finding grey hairs whenever she looked in the mirror.

The tapping on the door continued, despite the early hour. The lights being on must have alerted someone to her presence, but could anyone's need for cappuccino or cake really be that desperate?

Sandy was relieved to see a familiar figure and unlocked the door.

"I'm so sorry to trouble you." Penelope Harlow said, stepping inside. She was bundled into an expensive looking raincoat and her familiar designer wellies dripped mud on the floor. "I saw the light, hope you don't mind?"

"Of course not. Is everything OK?" Sandy asked.

"Yes, yes... I need to let you down, I'm afraid. I won't be able to do the story group this morning."

"Oh." Sandy said. Every Sunday morning, Penelope hosted a free children's story group in the shop. It was popular with locals and holidaymakers alike, and while the children enjoyed the group while sitting in a circle, their parents bought cake and books. It made Sundays one of the most profitable days of the week for Sandy, while many other local businesses didn't even open.

"I do hate letting you down, dear."

"It's ok, don't worry, Penelope. Is everything OK?" Sandy asked. Penelope had never let her down in the two years they had been running the story time, and come to think of it Sandy didn't think she had ever broken any other commitments she had. She was a woman who lived for community life.

Penelope let out a small sigh. "Yes. I really am sorry, though. And I will be back next week, I can assure you."

Sandy smiled. "Well, there's just one question remaining."

"What is it?"

"Any tips for a novice storytime presenter?"

The flippant remark made Penelope smile, caused her to relax as the books had made Sandy relax a while earlier. "Just throw yourself into it dear, the more silly you can be the better. You'll be fabulous!"

Sandy laughed.

"I'll see you soon, good luck!" Penelope called, and with that, she gave Sandy an awkward cross between a hug and a peck on the cheek and left the shop.

Sandy waved goodbye to her as Penelope returned to her 4x4 and drove away, then went back to her bookshelves. The sight of them in order made Sandy's heart glad, but she had run out of time for books.

There was baking to do.

First, she checked the leftovers. There were half a cappuccino cake and most of a vanilla sponge, a few chocolate chip cookies, and one lonely coconut tart. Sandy believed it was bad luck to leave any cakes lonely and devoured the small cake standing over the counter in the kitchen. The naughtiness of a cake before 8am made her smile to herself.

She checked the ingredients and made lemon curd tarts, sifting flour into a bowl then rubbing in the chilled margarine and lard until the mixture became breadcrumb-like. She added 1 1/2 tablespoons of water to bind the mixture, then rolled it in the bowl into a stiff pastry. There was something therapeutic about making pastry. No matter how tasty the ready-made options were, Sandy would always opt to make her own. There were corners she would cut - she was a particular fan of anything that came ready-grated, even if it was more expensive. But pastry had to be done by her hands in her kitchen.

She floured the surface and rolled out the dough, cutting out 12 circles with a biscuit cutter and placing each one into a hole on her tart tin.

In a small bowl, she mixed lemon curd, margarine, sugar and an egg and beat the mixture together, then stirred in 2oz flour, 1/2 teaspoon of baking powder and a generous serving of grated lemon rind (grated by hand, even!). And then, her mystery ingredient. She ripped up a single mint leaf until it was in tiny pieces and her fingers smelt of the fresh herb, and added the pieces to the mix, giving it a good stir before adding some to each pastry case.

The tarts went in the oven for 20 minutes and Sandy tried to ignore how much her mouth was watering. Lemon curd tarts were one of her favourite treats. So much so, she had to limit how often she allowed herself to bake them and how often she allowed herself to sample the batch.

The front door opened, the bell jingling to announce someone's arrival.

Sandy walked out front just as Coral took a seat.

"Morning," Sandy said, wiping her hands with a tea towel.

"Y'alright sis? What's up?" Coral asked, not meeting her sister's gaze.

"I'm sorry about last night," Sandy said. "I had a real headache, an early night was just what I needed."

"Better now?" Coral asked, her brow furrowed in concern.

Sandy smiled. "Much better. What can I get you?"

"Are you open yet?"

Sandy stole a glance at her watch. "Not for another ten minutes, but since it's you."

"I'll have a black coffee, please."

Sandy made the drink and decided she would make herself one and join her sister. It wasn't often they had time alone together.

"You know, there was something I wanted to tell you."

"Ok," Sandy said, the nervous feeling in her stomach reappearing.

"I don't know if I told you, but I had CCTV fitted to the house a while ago."

"You mentioned it, wasn't it when there was that car broken in to?"

"Yeah, that was it. I'd forgotten it's there, to be honest, but I realised last night and I thought I'd have a look at it. It keeps the recordings for a month, it's a proper professional bit of kit, and it looks out over the side of my cottage because that way it catches the path."

Sandy waited. Her sister's stories always took a while to find their point; as if being paid per word had affected her speech.

"I never realised, Sand, but my camera covers Reginald's cottage."

"Have you checked it?"

"Stayed up most of the night watching it all. And, there's something on there, on the night he was killed."

"You're kidding? Have you told the police?"

"No, I wanted to tell you first."

"We have to tell the police, Coral. What does it show?"

"Well... it shows you."

"Me?"

Coral nodded. "It shows you going in his cottage, and about twenty minutes later coming back out."

"That's crazy, I didn't go to his cottage. I've never been in his cottage in my life!"

"I know that." Coral said, grabbing Sandy's hand.

"So, what..."

"I think you're being framed, Sandy. Whoever killed him, dressed like you to do it."

10

*B*ernice was happy to cover the morning shift on short notice but reluctant to present the story time. Thankfully, she was owed a favour by Poppy Sanders, who agreed to handle that part of the Sunday morning routine.

Sandy sprinted out of the door as soon as Bernice arrived, offering some feeble explanation of a family emergency. She ran across the green and hammered on the door of Coral's cottage.

"It was open," Coral said, appearing in the doorway. Sandy followed her into the cottage, which despite its traditional exterior was modern and high-spec inside. Coral led Sandy into the small kitchen, where a tiny breakfast bar with two stools was squeezed into the space. On the breakfast bar was Coral's laptop, open with a blank screen.

"Are you sure you want to see it?" Coral asked, gesturing to Sandy's shaking hands.

"I need to. I don't want to." Sandy clarified, taking a seat on one stool.

"Ok. Here goes." Coral said.

She fired up the laptop and it sprang into life, showing the screen Coral had left it on, a paused and grainy CCTV footage.

"Ok, let me just rewind this," Coral said, hitting keys. Sandy looked on, watching the screen jump and start.

"It's grainy." She said.

Coral stiffened next to her. "It's top of the range, this is practically police-level surveillance footage."

"Excellent," Sandy said as Coral stopped the footage. "I'm so pleased we have police-level surveillance footage showing me going into and out of Reginald's house."

"We're not showing this to anyone, Sand," Coral exclaimed. "I'm showing you and then this gets deleted."

"You can't delete it, it's evidence."

Coral pressed play, and Sandy watched the footage. It showed Coral's garden path, and the cottage opposite her path, where Reginald Halfman had lived until his untimely demise. There was no movement at all for a few minutes, and if it hadn't been for the time stamp in the top corner racing through the seconds and minutes, Sandy would have thought it was still paused.

Then, to her horror, she appeared on the screen. Her long dark hair and distinctive yellow mac were visible, and she was wearing dark trousers and stiletto shoes. Stiletto shoes! She glanced around before opening the gate and walking down Reginald's path, where she knocked on the front door. Reginald appeared at the door, smiled at her, and ushered her inside.

"Oh my God, the poor man had no idea," Sandy said, covering her mouth.

"Awful, isn't it."

"Whoever it is, he knew her."

"Well enough to let her in."

They continued to watch. After a few minutes, a cat ran down Coral's path, but other than that nothing else happened until Reginald's front door opened again. Slower this time, more cautiously.

The woman who appeared to be Sandy peered out and checked both directions, then slipped out of the house, pulling the door closed behind her. With her head bent low, she crept down the path, checked the street both ways, and then opened the gate and walked off camera.

Coral reached forward and paused the footage again.

"And there's nothing else?" Sandy asked.

"I've watched as much as I could, but I told you there's a month's footage. I watched the hours before and after this happened; nothing else happens. Nobody comes, nobody goes. Knock yourself out if you want to watch some."

"Can we watch that bit again?" Sandy asked.

"Sure," Coral said, rewinding the footage. She hit play again.

Despite herself, Sandy gasped when the woman appeared on screen again. "I know for sure it isn't me, and it still makes me think it's me."

"It was so spooky when I first saw it," Coral said. "Who do you think it could be?"

"I have no idea," Sandy said. "I feel so over my head with this. Someone's trying to set me up."

"Well, at least it's not anyone you're really close to."

"What makes you say that?"

"Did you see the shoes?"

"Stilettos."

"You never wear stilettos. Anyone who knows you well knows that."

"Good point."

"So, this person knew you well enough to get your coat and a wig, but not to know what you wear on your feet."

Sandy smiled. "I guess it should be some kind of comfort that it's nobody really close, but how could someone do this, Coral? How could someone kill a man, and pretend to be me?"

"Hold on," Coral said. "Do you think he thought it was you he was letting in?"

The thought made Sandy's stomach churn.

"I don't know what to think anymore."

She would have imagined Reginald knew he had upset her, but he had been so arrogant it was easy to imagine he would have opened that door, thought it was Sandy standing before him, and guessed she had come around to the brilliance of his plan.

"Sis, I think you should stay with me," Coral said. "Whoever this is, they really want you out of the way. Either by framing you or... or..."

"Killing me." Sandy finished. Her whole body shivered as she said the words, and Coral gripped her hands.

"Please, stay here."

Sandy nodded. "Okay."

The two embraced, and as they did, Sandy saw something move on the screen.

"Wait! What's that? Go back." She ordered.

Coral rewinded the footage a few minutes and they watched together as the screen was perfectly still.

"You must have imagined it," Coral said.

"I didn't." Sandy insisted, and just then she saw it again. A woman appeared on screen, walking past Reginald's cottage from the left-hand side of the screen, the direction in which the woman pretending to be Sandy had walked away. The woman dashed on, looking around as she did. She was dressed in dark trousers, stiletto shoes, and a fancy jacket. The outfit wasn't what Sandy was used to seeing the woman in, but she still recognised her. "It's Elaine Peters."

"Your neighbour? The widow?" Coral asked.

Sandy nodded.

"It could be a coincidence," Coral said, but Sandy shook her head. "I can't believe I missed this bit."

"Look how nervous she looks. She's hiding something. And that outfit isn't her at all."

Coral rewound the footage and they both watched again as Elaine appeared on screen, twitchy and fast moving.

"She had a grudge against Reginald Halfman," Sandy revealed.

"And one against you?"

"I didn't think so... but I'm not sure who I can trust anymore."

"What do we do now?"

"We have to play it cool. I'm going to find out more about Elaine Peters." Sandy said. She stood up and let herself out of Coral's cottage before her sister could say another word.

On her walk back to the shop, she tried not to look at Reginald's empty cottage, but couldn't help herself. She tried to imagine what would make a person visit someone else, their pockets armed with poison, and take their life. Then she stopped herself, thinking maybe she didn't want to understand that kind of mindset.

When she got back to the shop, she wasn't surprised to see the place crowded. It was story time, and she could hear the sing-song voice of Poppy Sanders, the butcher's wife. As a primary school teacher, Poppy was ideal for leading the group, although her characters were all a little sweet-as-sugar compared to Penelope Harlow's. Penelope was excellent at throwing herself into perfecting different voices, and the wicked witches and the snapping crocodiles were some of her most popular.

The crowd of parents she knew and didn't know seemed to all be spaced out on caffeine highs, enjoying the child-free peace, and she smiled at the fact that her little cafe could offer such bliss for people. It was a feeling she relished.

"Everything ok?" Bernice asked, emerging from the kitchen with a full English breakfast which she presented in front of a woman Sandy didn't recognise.

"All good now, thanks for covering."

"Anytime. Shall I stick around?"

"No," Sandy said. "I'll take it from here."

"If you're sure," Bernice said, taking her apron off. "I think I'm going to go shopping."

"Enjoy," Sandy called, watching until Bernice had left.

She turned her attention to the cafe and was pleased to see Dorie Slaughter in her usual seat, a huge slab of cappuccino cake on a plate in front of her.

"How's the IBS, Dorie?" Sandy asked, approaching her with a fresh mug of tea to replace the woman's empty one.

"Ooh Sandy, do you know, all those vegetables upset it something chronic. I figure if I'm going to live in pain anyway, it might as well be worth it. Nice cake, by the way."

"I don't blame you," Sandy said, wondering how to veer the subject around to Elaine Peters. If anyone knew about the village goings-on, it was Dorie Slaughter.

"Is that for me? You're a good 'un." Dorie said, gesturing to the mug of tea.

"I have to look after my best customer," Sandy said. The compliment made the woman sit up with pride. "Although, I have to say there's competition."

"Competition?"

"Elaine Peters. Hardly see her in years and then she seems to be in here all the time."

"Hmm." Dorie murmured. "She's got a new lease of life, hasn't she."

"It's nice to see... after what she went through."

"She knows loss, that woman," Dorie said, the sentiment choking her up. Dorie was a widow herself, although she had been widowed for so long that it was easier to think of her as being single.

"So do you," Sandy said. "It must change you, losing your husband like that."

"It made me so angry," Dorie admitted. "If he hadn't been dead, I could have killed him myself for dying on me."

Sandy placed a supportive hand on Dorie's shoulder. "I wonder if Elaine felt like that. Angry."

"She did," Dorie said, then appeared to regret the words. "It's not my place to say, of course."

"I didn't realise you really knew her."

"We attend the same support group."

"Support group? I didn't even know we had such a thing here, forgive my ignorance."

"We have to go to the next village. It's a bereavement group, I call it the Black Widows' Club. Full of women who are angry that their husbands dared to die."

"Sounds, erm, supportive."

"Well, Elaine stopped going a few weeks ago. Said it wasn't the right group for her. Said she needed a different, what did she say... needed some other way of getting closure."

"I hope she got it," Sandy said, hardly able to contain the bitterness in her voice. The thought of Elaine using her to gain closure for herself, no matter how she had been hurt in the past, made Sandy's stomach-churning turn into real, physical pain.

"Are you ok, dear? You look a little pale."

"I think I"m just hungry, I skipped breakfast. Good job I work in a cafe, hey." Sandy joked, then walked away from Dorie's table and retreated into the kitchen. She pulled her notebook out of her handbag, turned to her page of investigation notes and wrote Elaine's name in large capital letters, then circled it in a heavy black pen.

The thought of Elaine in a coat identical to her own, walking out of Reginald's house before disappearing off camera where she must have discarded the yellow coat and replaced it with a fancy one, replayed in her mind throughout the day.

It was an especially busy day as the rain poured without end and people tried to hide out from it for as long as possible.

Sandy tried to focus on her customers but whenever she had a quiet moment, she found her mind returning to the CCTV footage and the feeling of dread returned to her stomach.

11

"*A*re you coming to mine?" Coral asked, her voice frantic. It was twenty minutes after closing time and Sandy was still in the shop, finishing washing the pots.

"Yep, if that's ok, I'm going to finish up here and then grab some things from home. I can pick up a takeaway on my way over if you fancy?"

"I'd love a bag of chips," Coral said. "Don't be too long, I'm famished."

"Leave it with me, text me your order."

Sandy finished the last few pots, grateful that she had retreated into the kitchen to do batches throughout the day instead of letting them all pile up until closing time. Then she surveyed the remaining cakes. Almost everything had sold out. She would have to be in early again the next day to bake a fresh selection.

There were two lemon curd tarts left, and although they weren't lonely together, Sandy decided she had earned a special treat, and slipped them both into her handbag in a paper bag.

She locked up and got in her car, then drove the short distance home.

Her cottage was in darkness, and she cursed herself for not leaving a light on when she had left. She let herself in, then locked the door behind her and headed straight up the stairs into her bedroom, where she pulled her never-used gym bag out from underneath the bed. She threw some clothes into it, several pairs of underwear, some toiletries and the novel she had been reading for weeks. When things went back to normal, she would love to spend a whole day relaxing with a book.

She was ready to leave when a light tap on the front door made her jump.

She peered out of her bedroom window but couldn't see down to the door below. Listening to the sinking feeling in her stomach, she ignored the knock and remained out of sight by the window.

After a few moments, she watched as Elaine Peters backed away from the door, looking up and straight into Sandy's bedroom window. Sandy, hiding behind the curtains, was confident she couldn't be seen, but still, her heart raced in her chest.

A second later she heard the click of someone walking, and looked down to see Elaine walking back down her path, her feet in stiletto shoes.

**

"We need to call the police," Coral said after Sandy had finished recounting what had just happened. "She was obviously going to try to kill you again."

"We can't tell the police," Sandy said. "I'm safe here. I just need to be careful."

"Just be careful? That's your plan?"

"And I need to find proof."

"The CCTV is proof!"

"No, the CCTV shows me entering and leaving Reginald's house, and Elaine Peters walking past a few minutes later."

"But it isn't you."

"Of course I'd say that," Sandy said. "She's trapped me."

"I can't believe you forgot the chips," Coral said, attempting to lighten the mood. She nudged Sandy with her bony elbow, but her joke fell flat. "Hey, sis, come on, we'll work something out."

"Of course we will, we're the Shaw Sisters." Sandy said, forcing herself to act as if she meant her words. She didn't want Coral to know how much it had unnerved her seeing Elaine standing on her doorstep in those garish stiletto shoes.

"If we can get through life with seaside names in a village nowhere near the sea, we can get through this." Coral laughed.

"Do you remember the teasing?" Sandy asked.

"Of course I do. I remember one lad asking me if there was a third sister called Dolphin!"

"Dolphin? It was Octopus when I went to upper school."

"To be fair, I think I know what the third daughter would have been called..."

"Mermaid!" They both said in unison, descending into wild laughter. Their parents had been hippies at heart, harboring dreams of life by the sea that they had never turned into reality.

"What do you think they'd make of all this?" Sandy asked,.

"Oh, that's an easy one. They'd say a mind does its best thinking on a full stomach. Come on, let's get those chips."

**

The Village Fryer was a few doors down from Books and Bakes and was a new addition to the village's array of shops.

Judging by its popularity most nights, it was hard to imagine what people had done for dinner before it opened.

"Oh, hello," Bernice said, standing behind the counter in a white apron and hairnet.

Sandy looked at her aghast. "Bernice? What are you doing here?"

"I think she's frying fish, Sand. I guess I got the brains, hey."

"Fish, sausages, you name it, I fry it," Bernice said, but her voice was high-pitched. "What can I do you?"

"Bernice, what are you doing working here?" Sandy asked, then gasped. "This is because I cut your hours, isn't it?"

"Look, love, it's fine. A few hours here, a few hours there, it all adds up."

"I thought you were glad to have a rest," Sandy said, realising why Bernice had been so keen to step in and help at short notice. Not to mention why she had asked today if she was needed to hang around for longer. She needed the money.

"I am, pet, but the bills don't pay themselves and our Mike isn't earning like he used to."

"You should have said," Sandy said.

"I couldn't do that. If I'd told you, you'd have given me my hours back and struggled yourself and that's not right. We need that business of yours to keep doing well, and if that means I have some shifts here when it's quiet over there, I can handle that."

"You shouldn't worry about the shop, Bernice, that's my job."

"Excuse me." Bernice said, standing straighter. "When you hired me, it became my job to worry about Books and Bakes. We're a team. Now, enough of this, what can I get for you?"

"Well I'm starving, I'll have chips and a sausage," Coral said, and Sandy was grateful for her larger-than-life sister who had bundles more confidence than she did.

"Make that two. I'll have curry on mine." Sandy said.

"Curry? You animal!" Coral exclaimed, and they all laughed.

Bernice prepared the order to go, and they walked back down the high street in a comfortable silence, each tucking into their dinner.

"It's been ages since I had a chip supper," Sandy admitted.

"Clearly, that's why you didn't know about Bernice."

"You mean you did?"

"Yeah, she served me the same order a few days ago. I've got a real love for a bag of chips."

"Why didn't you tell me?" Sandy asked.

Coral shrugged. "I didn't see it as news, to be honest. A local woman works in a chip shop! Hardly a tabloid exclusive, is it?"

"I guess. I just wish I could afford to pay her for enough to save her working two jobs."

"You will do sis, chin up. You said it was mad today."

"It was." Sandy agreed. "Let's hope it stays that way."

"Why don't you do more events?" Coral asked. Sandy looked at her, unable to answer due to the bite of sausage she had just taken. "You say Sundays are busy because of the story time, why not do more things like that?"

"Another story time?"

"Not exactly... Penelope Harlow's terrifying witch voice once a week is often enough. But how about a monthly book club, or even late opening nights?"

"I had thought about a late opening, but I'm reluctant to be in the shop late at night with what's going on."

"Well, there's only one thing for it then."

"What's that?"

"We need to catch Elaine Peters, and then we can move on with our lives."

"I'll, erm, eat to that." Sandy joked, and the two of them skewered their sausages on their plastic forks and held them up as if making a toast.

The village looked so peaceful as they strolled across the village square that it was surreal to remember what had been happening over the last few days. It was perfectly quiet, despite being only early evening still, and the lamp-posts illuminated the pretty cottages.

Sandy could see Coral's cottage up ahead and forced her gaze to linger on it and only it, ignoring Reginald's cottage that stood in darkness across the road.

Sandy stopped walking and stood still underneath a lamppost, surveying the village green.

She had been tempted to refuse the walk out to the chip shop, wanting nothing more than to hide away in her sister's safe home, but she was glad she had ventured out. She loved Waterfell Tweed, and she wouldn't let anyone or anything change that.

Sandy remembered the lemon curd tarts in her handbag and pulled the brown paper bag out, holding it in the air for Coral to see.

"What's that?" She asked, walking closer to Sandy for a better look.

"Pudding." Sandy declared. "Last one home can make the drinks."

It took Coral a moment to react when Sandy took off running across the green, but then she was on her tail. Coral had always been the fastest, the fittest, the one who paid for a gym membership and used it. The slight head start shouldn't have been enough to allow Sandy to win.

But she ran with a determination she had never felt in PE classes or since. Now, she found that she was at Coral's front door while her sister was still running across the damp grass. She was out of breath, her heartbeat banging in her ears, and to her surprise, the adrenaline felt good. She crouched over and a sudden jolt of stitch hit her left side, causing her to moan in pain.

"Well played, little sis," Coral said, as she breezed up to the door, without so much as appearing out of breath.

"You let me win, you toad," Sandy said, in between pants.

"You can't prove that. Come on, I'll make the drinks."

or the first night in the last week, Sandy slept like a log. She collapsed into a deep slumber as soon as her head hit the pillow just after 9pm, and didn't wake up until she heard Coral turn on the shower in the bathroom.

She opened her eyes, feeling as though she could sleep for another several hours. There was no alarm clock by the bedside in Coral's spare room, in fact, there was nothing more than a bed and a few boxes of paperwork and other junk that called the spare room home.

Sandy reached down for her phone and saw with horror that it was 8am. She dived out of bed but realised she was trapped until Coral finished in the shower, as she couldn't leave without at least a basic wash. She closed her eyes, just for a moment, and then woke with a jolt twenty minutes later.

Panicked, she burst out of the spare room to find Coral sitting in her bedroom, straightening her hair in an relaxed manner.

"Do you know what time it is? We're both going to be

late!" Sandy exclaimed, darting past her into her bathroom. There was no time for a shower, she'd have to just strip and scrub herself at the sink.

"I have nowhere to be." Coral called. "I'm not at work today."

"I need you to come with me, then." Sandy called from within the bathroom. "Please, Coral, come and serve for me while I bake? I could really do with a hand."

She heard Coral laugh from her bedroom but hoped she would realise the request was serious. As bad as Sandy felt for Bernice needing a second job, she had already called her in for more extra hours for the month than she could afford.

She brushed her teeth, gave herself a quick wash, then brushed her hair and applied deodorant. Anything else would have to wait for another day.

She opened the bathroom door, to find that Coral's bedroom was empty.

She shook her head, resigning herself to a busy day of managing the counter and baking the cakes, and made her way downstairs.

Standing by the door, already in her little pixie boots and coat, was Coral.

"Come on, sis, you said we were late." She said with a grin, then added. "I hope you know what you're letting yourself in for."

**

Coral was a complete mess in the kitchen, putting things in the wrong place and breaking every rule of food hygiene, especially when she saw the mixture for the red velvet cake that Sandy was making and stuck a finger in to have a taste. She carried the dirty pots one at a time, instead of the piled and balanced towers that Sandy and Bernice carried to save time. And she spent a lot more time texting on her phone than Sandy would allow if she was paying her.

But, Coral was an absolute winner with the customers. While Sandy's shyness meant she took the orders as they were given, it turned out that Coral was an expert saleswoman.

"You're liking that book, hey?" She said to one man, who was sitting at a table in the cafe working his way through a book on antiques while eating a full breakfast. "Let me ring this through the counter for you, save you a job for later."

And with that, she had taken his money for a book he may well have planned to browse and leave behind. He looked utterly startled but didn't protest.

Sandy shook her head in amazement.

For the entire morning, not a single customer had only a drink. They would place their order for a tea, or a cappuccino, and Coral would reply, "And to eat?"

Sandy was certain that some of the first-time visitors thought it was mandatory to order food!

"You're amazing!" Sandy whispered as Coral appeared in the kitchen with a single used plate.

"Oh stop, no, tell me more." Coral joked, but she was enjoying herself.

"You need to tell me your secrets."

"People are in here to spend money, Sandy, just help them!" She said, as if it was that simple, and then returned to her public out front.

Sandy moved to the counter and watched her work her magic.

Jim Slaughter was ordering a coffee to go.

"And which cake shall I pack for you to save for lunch?" Coral asked.

Jim, never one to disobey a direct request, was an easy target, but Sandy would never dare ask the question.

"Erm, I'll take two slices of the hazelnut torte." He said, then spotted Sandy. "Are you hiding?"

"Busy baking." She said, moving forward and cutting two slabs of the torte for him, placing each one in a separate brown paper bag. "I overslept this morning."

"That's not like you. Are you feeling okay?"

"I'm good, thanks for asking." She said, taking his money and ringing the order in the till. "I hope you and your mum enjoy the cake."

"Oh," Jim said, his cheeks flushing red. "Yes, yes... thank you."

"He's a strange man," Coral said, the second he was gone.

"He's harmless," Sandy said. "But he's not sharing that cake with his mother."

Coral laughed. "Dorie Slaughter is the only woman in his life, she always has been."

"Not true. Dorie hinted herself that he's found love."

"Oh dear, I pity the woman who has to compete with Dorie for first place in his eyes."

"Coral!" Sandy scalded, then returned to the kitchen. The red velvet cake was in the oven, she had already made the hazelnut torte, and she was about to make fruit scones. She always had plenty of thick double cream and strawberry jam, and seeing those in the fridge made her fancy eating a scone piled high with lashings of them on. Sometimes, the best reason to bake a particular cake was that she felt like eating some of it herself.

She busied herself with the ingredients, keeping an ear

out for Coral's sales techniques, smiling to herself. It was nice having her sister around.

**

Sandy could hardly believe that the till total was genuine.

"We've made more than double today what I did yesterday!" Sandy said, pulling a few notes from the pile and holding them out for Coral.

"What are you doing?"

"Take it, you've been an absolute lifesaver today."

"I haven't done it because I want money, sis," Coral said.

"I know that, but please, we've done really well and, you're letting me stay with you, you're doing so much..."

"Oh, please. Put it away." Coral insisted. "You're my sister. And, truth be told, I've had a blast today. It's been a few years since I've worked in retail, I'd forgotten how much I enjoyed it."

"Don't suppose you want to be my Saturday girl, do you?" Sandy half-joked.

"I'll help you out anytime, and sure, I don't mind pulling a few shifts to get things moving. But I do nothing you and Bernice couldn't do, it's not magic. I see it as a challenge to make sure nobody leaves empty-handed."

"You want them to have empty wallets, not empty hands!" Sandy said with a laugh. She was washing the dishes, while Coral stood at the counter eating a scone.

"Well, it's better for you that way isn't it," Coral said, in between bites. "Mmm, this is so good. How did you get the baking gene?"

"You got the beautiful-hair-like-mum gene," Sandy said, gesturing to Coral's deep red hair. She had hated the colour as a child, but ever since she transformed into a beautiful teenager, Coral had adored her hair colour and wore it well.

"True." She admitted. "So, Elaine Peters didn't show her face today."

"Thankfully."

"How do you think we're going to get proof?"

"I keep thinking a bright idea will come to me, but nothing yet."

"My best ideas come to me in the shower," Coral said.

"Well, I'd better wake up earlier in the morning tomorrow then."

**

The shower wasn't needed.

The idea came to Sandy as she walked home with Coral that afternoon.

"I've got it." She said, waving at Bernice who was in the chip shop again.

"What? I can't have fish and chips again!"

"No, I've got it. I know how to get proof. I'm going to show Elaine the CCTV."

"Are you insane?" Coral asked, stopping and facing Sandy. Her eyes were full of concern.

"I'm going to confront her, show her only the bit showing her walking past, so she won't know that I know she tried to set me up. I'll offer to help her, to keep her secret, and I'll really be recording her."

"That sounds really dangerous," Coral said. "dangerous."

"There's no other way," Sandy said. "In fact, I'm going to do it tonight. I can't wait any longer."

**

Coral insisted on driving Sandy to Elaine's house and remaining outside in the car, although Sandy wasn't sure what good she thought she would do from out there.

Coral had had to edit the CCTV clip and send the small clip showing only Elaine reappearing to Sandy's mobile.

"You promise me you'll be safe? If anything goes wrong, come and stand by the window and I'll call the police straight away." Coral said, her hands shaking on the steering wheel. She had parked a couple of houses away and had already shut the headlights off so the car was in darkness.

"I'll be fine, Coral, don't worry." Sandy said, hoping her words sounded more convincing than they felt. She gave Coral a kiss on the cheek, then opened the passenger door and got out.

The cold night air hit her, causing her to do a sharp intake of breath. She pulled her yellow mac tighter around her, then walked toward Elaine's cottage.

She knocked on the door three times, aiming for a knock somewhere between aggressive and timid. The living room light was on, but the curtains were drawn. So much for Coral's plan of appearing in the window to signal for help. She couldn't hear anything within the cottage for a few seconds and wondered if Elaine was even in.

"Who is it?" Elaine called then.

"It's me, Sandy. Can I come in?"

Elaine laughed from inside. "Oh yes, dear."

She unbolted the door and held it open, allowing Sandy to enter. Sandy hadn't been in Elaine's home for some time. Since Elaine had withdrawn from village life she had always answered the door and accepted delivery of parcels and remained neighbourly, but there had been no invitations over for dinner as there had been years before. Elaine lead Sandy into the living room, where a small lamp was lit and a candle was burning on the coffee table. Classical music played.

"Can I get you a drink?

"Ooh, a cup of tea would be wonderful, please." Sandy said, stalling for time. Elaine smiled and left the room, padding down the corridor to the kitchen.

While she was alone in the room, Sandy took the chance to look around. It was a perfectly normal living room. A fresh bunch of flowers stood in a vase by the hearth, and a photograph of Elaine on her wedding day stood atop the mantelpiece. Her late husband was absent on the photo.

"Here you go," Elaine said, returning to the room quicker than Sandy expected, while she was still standing up and looking at the wedding photograph.

"You have such a beautiful home, Elaine."

"Do you need something, Sandy?" Elaine asked, placing the tea on a mat on the coffee table.

"I need to show you something," Sandy said, taking her phone from her pocket. She found the video clip and gestured for Elaine to come and sit by her, which she did. "This is CCTV showing the outside of Reginald's cottage on the evening he was killed."

Elaine gulped.

The footage played, and Elaine appeared on screen, looking nervous and in a rush.

"That's you, isn't it?" Sandy asked.

"Well, it's grainy." Elaine said. The flush in her cheeks told Sandy that she had recognised herself. "Is there any more?"

"This is all we've found at the moment. I have to present

it to the police, you know that. This places you as the last person to go near Reginald's cottage."

"I don't know what you mean, it's not a crime to walk past a house."

"It isn't, but look how nervous you look, Elaine. I think the police will wonder why you looked so nervous."

Elaine opened her mouth to speak, but there was a sudden noise from the back room. Elaine jumped up and Sandy moved away from her, to the window. She hadn't managed to pull the curtains open when a man appeared in the doorway.

"Elaine." He said, cloaked in darkness from the hallway. "Let me deal with this."

Sandy tried to reach behind her to find the curtain parting, without taking her eyes off the man in the doorway, but her attempts were in vain.

The man moved into the room, revealing his identity, and Sandy gasped.

"Jim!" She exclaimed.

"Sandy." He replied, walking over to Elaine so they stood so close to each other they almost touched. "Sit down."

Sandy moved away from the window and reclaimed the same spot on the settee.

"I can explain everything," Jim said.

"Jim, don't." Elaine pleaded.

"We have to, Elaine." He said, sounding more assertive than Sandy had ever heard.

"You can tell me," Sandy said, attempting to reassure them that she was on side. When she made her plan, she had been confident that she could fight Elaine off if necessary, and she hadn't taken a single sip of her tea. She had never expected there would be two of them.

"Elaine was nervous, you're right," Jim admitted, and to

Sandy's horror he turned to Elaine and smiled. "But she was with me."

"You're not on the CCTV," Sandy said.

"She'd left me by then, but I can vouch for her whereabouts before then."

"Are you saying it wasn't you?" Sandy asked Elaine. She had been certain that, confronted alone, the woman would confess. She'd read an article about killers years before that said they all wanted to be caught deep down, and she'd remembered that when she hatched this plan.

"Of course it wasn't me, Sandy!" Elaine exclaimed, her eyes wide with horror at being accused. "How could you think such a thing?"

Sandy gulped, losing her nerve. "I didn't think it, I came to show you the CCTV and ask you about it. Give you chance to explain."

Jim sighed. "The truth is..."

"Let me." Elaine said, placing a hand on Jim's arm. She sat down on the settee opposite the one Sandy was sitting on, and Jim sat beside her. "Sandy, Jim and I have been dating."

"Dating?"

Elaine nodded. "It's still early days, but we're having a wonderful time together."

"We really are." Jim agreed, and Sandy realised who the second slice of torte had been for. He looked smitten. "Elaine was with me the day Reginald was killed, we went out of town for lunch and a movie. It was an off day for me."

"Why do you look so nervous on the footage?" Sandy asked.

Elaine gave a small laugh. "Jim had dropped me off a few doors away and I was nervous someone might have seen."

"Why, is it a secret?"

Elaine's face fell and she whispered. "There are times I feel so guilty I cancel plans to see him."

Jim squeezed her hand. "I know how losing a husband never really leaves you, I watched my mum go through it. We spent our first date getting to know each other and I heard as much about Martin as about Elaine. I can handle the broken plans and the guilt, she's worth it."

"But we can't handle the gossip, not yet," Elaine said, her eyes damp with tears. "I can work a way through my own judgement, but not other people's."

"What are you scared of?" Sandy asked, realising that her suspicions were entirely false. She had caught a woman in love, not a killer.

"I don't want anyone to think I'm disrespecting my husband's memory. I couldn't handle that."

"Is that the reason for the photograph?" Sandy asked, and Elaine's cheeks flushed.

"Yes. I can't believe I've done that to him." Elaine said, breaking down in tears. The same words she'd said to Dorie Slaughter in the cafe. How foolish Sandy felt. She had overheard two widows discussing moving forward with their lives. "The photo of me reminds me that I'm married, comforts me on the bad days. But I'm not strong enough to see his face every day. Not when I'm laughing and joking with Jim, I can't manage that."

"You know Elaine, it doesn't matter what anyone else thinks. If you feel ready, and this feels right, that's it. And I think everyone in the village would be pleased for you."

"We will tell people." Jim blurted. "But not yet. Not until Elaine is sure she is ready."

"I just felt so silly that night," Elaine said with a sigh. "I had no idea Reginald had been killed. I'd had the most wonderful time with Jim, and then there I was doing the walk of shame in those silly shoes. I decided on the walk home to call it a day,, I felt so strange about it all. And then I heard the news, and I realised how much I wanted to give it a go, for real."

"And that's what we're doing," Jim said, with a smile. "It feels like being a teenager again, sneaking around, but I kind of like it."

"I think you make a lovely couple," Sandy said, and she meant it. Jim was such a gentleman, an easy-going gentle soul who had been overpowered all his life by his mother. It was nice to see him with a woman as gentle as he was. Sandy remembered her earlier belief that Elaine was the murderer and felt her cheeks flush with shame.

"So do we," Jim said, beaming at her with pride.

"Thank you for coming over and showing me the footage, Sandy," Elaine said. "I appreciate you giving me the chance to explain. I know you still have to let the police see it for themselves."

Sandy pulled the phone out of her pocket and held the screen up to them both as she clicked delete. "There, it's gone. As you said, it's hardly a crime walking past a house."

Elaine let out a long breath in relief. "Thank you."

Jim looked at the floor, no doubt debating whether or not the footage had been evidence.

"Sandy, I've been trying to speak to you for a couple of days. I wanted you to know that I know you're innocent. If there's anything I can do to help, I'm always here for you." Elaine said.

Elaine's belief in her, a belief that she hadn't been able to return, made Sandy's eyes fill with tears. "Thanks, Elaine, I appreciate that. I've been staying with Coral for a few days, but I think it's time to come home."

Elaine nodded. "I moved out, you know, when it first happened. I hadn't been alone in a house overnight for years, and I was scared to be. I went to stay with my parents, and it was wonderful really as they looked after me and cooked my meals and washed my clothes. But I stayed too long. It's important, to come home."

Sandy nodded and stood up. "You're right."

She said her goodbyes and let herself out of the cottage, not wanting to intrude on the couple's time together any further. It was pouring with rain and she ran across to Coral's car, where her sister sat awaiting the news.

"Well?" She asked.

Sandy gave one last look at the cottage and the secrets it contained. "It's not her."

13

*I*t was nice to wake up in her own cottage again, even if she had only been away for a couple of days. There were sounds that only her cottage made as it woke up in the morning, and she had never realised before what a comfort those sounds were to her.

She lay in bed, the thick mattress wrapped around her, and listened to the water drip in the pipes and churn in the tank as it heated up for the day.

It was 6am, she had woken just before her alarm went off so had switched it off before it started. She always thought that alarm clock alerts were an awful noise to wake up to in the world.

It was dark outside still, and the bedroom was cool when she jumped out of the bed covers. She padded across to the bathroom and jumped straight in a hot shower, enjoying the too warm water on her skin.

Her thoughts turned to Elaine and Jim, and how in love they were, even if they were not admitting it to themselves or other people yet. The thought made her smile to herself.

Arriving at Books and Bakes, she followed her usual

morning routine of turning on the radio and checking the leftover cakes, then threw herself into a new experiment: a rainbow sponge cake. The recipe was simple; five different sponge cakes, each one dyed with a different food colouring, to produce a rainbow collection of sponges that would be piled high and sandwiched with strawberries and cream.

She made yellow, blue, green, orange and red sponges and left them to bake, turning her attention to a tray of chocolate flapjack. Flapjack was her earliest baking memory, back when she was at school. She remembered her mum weighing the ingredients out the night before and placing each one in a separate brown paper bag, so that all Sandy had to do was add them at the right time. The flapjacks had turned out delicious in Sandy's opinion, and Sandy had become convinced that she had a great future ahead of her in the culinary kitchens of the world. When the teacher had declared that her flapjack was not quite moist enough, Sandy's dreams were ruined and she had sulked with her mum for several days for not sending her with enough golden syrup.

The memory made her smile as she greased a square tin and lined it with parchment paper, then set to work melting butter, sugar and syrup. The smell of warm, melted butter was one of her favourite things about baking, and she inhaled deeply. Oats were next, sprinkled in by hand and then stirred through until mixed well, and then she added some chocolate chips.

Sandy then transferred the whole mixture spoon by spoon into the tin and baked for 15 minutes.

Sandy stood back and allowed herself a moment to relax, then unlocked the front door and prepared for another day.

**

Tuesday was always a quiet day for the shop. Many of the village shops closed for the day because of how quiet it was, which had the effect of making it an even quieter day for the shops that remained open.

A few customers wandered in during the morning for a drink or a browse. Sandy sold five books, feeling that familiar buzz of excitement with each purchase made.

There was plenty of quiet time in-between, though, and Sandy filled that by continuing with sorting out the books. She still had a storage unit out of town half-full with enough books to fill another shop, and she didn't know what to do with the books or the unit. Her heart told her to expand the books, but the only way of doing that would be to remove the cafe area, which would lose her valuable income.

Her thoughts were disturbed by the bell jingling to announce that there was a customer. She dusted her hands off on her trousers and went to greet them.

"Good afternoon," Sandy said, approaching the cafe area to see Penelope and Benedict Harlow at the counter, gazing at the menu.

"Hello, Sandy, how was story time? I'm so sorry again, to let you down." Penelope said, and Sandy wondered how long she would continue to apologise for.

"It's fine Penelope, I told you not to worry. It was busy as always."

"And did you enjoy it, dear?"

"Oh! I didn't do it. I had to run an errand - Poppy Sanders stepped in."

"The teacher? I bet she did a fabulous job!"

"I hear it went down well," Sandy said, not wanting

Penelope to think that Poppy had been better than her. The story time sessions were a highlight for the village children, but for her tills as well, and she needed that busy time each week to make up for days like Tuesdays.

"It's very quiet," Benedict said as if reading her mind. The only other customer was Cass, who was enjoying a salad on her lunch break from her salon. "You are open, aren't you?"

"Of course. Tuesdays are always like this. Why don't you take a seat and I'll come over in a second?"

The couple nodded and chose a table by the window while Sandy retreated into the kitchen to wash her hands and put on her apron.

"Two ham salads, please," Benedict ordered for them both when Sandy returned to their table.

"And I'll have an Earl Grey," Penelope added.

"Ah, same for me," Benedict said.

"Of course," Sandy said. "I don't mean to pry, but is everything ok?"

The Harlows glanced at each other.

"Nothing we can't resolve, dear," Penelope said after a few moments. "Thank you for asking."

Sandy wasn't sure what problems the Harlow family could have, with their inherited fortune, manor house and popularity, but she knew it wasn't her place to judge.

In the kitchen, she prepared three ham salads, served two to the Harlows and sat down at Cass' table with the third for herself.

"Enjoying that?" Sandy asked, gesturing to the salad that had hardly been touched on Cass' plate.

"I try to eat salads," Cass said. "But when it's so cold, all you need is a big cottage pie."

"Do you remember when we used to do things like that here?"

Cass' eyes grew wide. "Do I? Of course, I do! I lived for Bernice's pies. Can't you do that again, Sand?"

"I can when I have staff again. I can't manage the front of house, all of the baking and then savoury things to cook as well. Jacket potatoes are the limit, just toss them in and forget them."

Cass nodded. "Do you think things will get better?"

"I hope so," Sandy said. "I keep thinking that more books are the key. At the moment it's such a little bookshop, nobody out of town knows about me. But if I had more space for books, word would get out and people would come especially for Books and Bakes."

"Maybe they'd have their nails done while they're here," Cass said with a smile.

"Are you quiet too?" Sandy asked. It was unusual for Cass to close the salon for a lunch break.

"I'm ticking over. I'm going to start microblading, that should get some new business in."

"What on earth is microblading?"

"Semi-permanent eyebrows, they're almost tattooed on," Cass said, inspecting her friend's bushy eyebrows too closely. "You should try it."

"Nobody is tattooing my eyebrows. Not even you, Cass."

"Come over and have them waxed at least? It doesn't even hurt."

Sandy pursed her lips. Ever since school, Cass had been the glamorous one. She had gone through a blue eyeshadow stage while Sandy was still playing with dolls. On nights out, when they had got ready together, Sandy had washed her face and self-consciously dusted some blusher over her cheeks and dabbed the mascara wand across her eyelashes, while Cass set out a terrifying amount of beauty products and set about transforming not only the look, but the shape, of her face.

"What do I look like?" She had asked on one such occasion, appearing from the bathroom looking all sallowed cheeks and slimline nose.

"Honestly?" Sandy had asked. "A skeleton."

"Perfect, that's the plan." Cass had replied, returning to the bathroom for twenty more minutes to finalise the look. She had gone out that night with the most perfect, and false, bone structure on her face.

It was like magic to Sandy. Magic she could admire, but magic she didn't particularly want to play a role in her own life.

"Well?" Cass asked, jolting Sandy back to the present moment.

"Sorry, I was miles away," Sandy admitted, smiling at her friend and realising how amazing it was that they had grown into such different people but remained so close.

"Eyebrow waxing? I was saying I'll do the first one free for you."

Sandy let out a small laugh. She had noticed that her eyebrows were looking a little out of control. "Go on then, but you have to be gentle with me. And don't think it's waxing this week and microtattooing next week!"

"Microtattooing? You're hilarious. I do love you, Sand."

Cass' sudden affection made Sandy think back to the argument she had overheard. She had trusted that Cass would tell her about when she was ready, but her friend had remained closed-lipped about it.

"You know, if there was anything going on, any problems, you could tell me," Sandy said, eyeing Cass. She was about to put a fork of lettuce into her mouth but stopped at Sandy's words.

"Of course I could." Cass said, narrowing her eyes, unsure where the comment had come from. "I tell you everything."

"I think I've realised these last few days that nobody tells anyone everything," Sandy said. "And it's often the things we most need the support of a good friend for, that we keep to ourselves."

"Are you ok, Sand?" Cass asked, returning her fork to the table.

Sandy nodded. "I just want you to know you can tell me anything."

Cass shifted in her seat. "I'd better get back to the salon. Thanks for a lovely lunch, and for looking out for me."

"I could pop over tonight and see you?" Sandy offered.

"I'm going to have an early night, to be honest," Cass said, standing up and putting her coat on. "I'm still getting tired."

"Of course," Sandy said, knowing that that was true. She had never seen Cass yawn as much as she had since her attack and while she didn't understand the details of how a bang to the head would cause so much tiredness, the two seemed to go hand in hand. She stood up and embraced Cass, then watched her leave the shop and return across the square to her salon.

"I thought she'd never leave." Benedict said after a moment.

"Benedict!" Penelope scalded.

"Oh no, she's a painted delight!" Benedict said, with a laugh. "We wanted to catch you alone, Sandy, that's all. It's why we came in today."

"Oh, I see. Shall I get us all another drink?"

Sandy made the drinks, then pulled up another chair and sat down with the Harlows.

"We'd like to ask you a favour," Benedict asked.

Sandy tried to hide her surprise. The Harlows never asked favours.

"It's not really a favour, darling. We have a project we'd like you to work with us on."

"Tell me more," Sandy said.

"We're going to host a Winter Ball. We've talked about one for years and never quite found the right time, but with what has happened in the village, we thought now might be the time it's most needed."

"It sounds wonderful," Sandy said. "But you do know there's a murderer on the loose still?"

"Nothing unites like a common enemy," Benedict said. "I say we stand in defiance. We eat, drink and be merry. That's what the spirit of Waterfell Tweed is all about."

"Ok. And where do I come in?"

"Catering, of course. We'll set up a marquee at the manor, and you can sort the buffet."

"When are you thinking? And how many people?"

"That's the thing," Penelope said. "We want to do it next week."

"Next week?"

"Is that a problem?" Benedict asked.

"It's not a problem for me," Sandy said. "It could be an issue with the suppliers. And, I'd have to find staff. My kitchen might not be big enough."

"We can sort all of those things," Penelope said. "City suppliers will be used to large orders at short notice, and you can use the manor kitchen to prepare. Have all of the food delivered to us, the housekeeper will take delivery and it will all be ready for you."

Sandy grinned. She had seen the manor kitchen once before, when delivering a cake for a birthday of Charlotte's. It was an incredible space, bigger than the whole of her shop, with every kitchen aid and tool she could ever have dreamt of. To prepare food in there must be a joy.

"What do you say?" Benedict asked.

"I say let's do it. It sounds like just what the village needs."

"Excellent!" Benedict said, clapping his hands together. "We have a busy day then, dear."

"We do indeed." Penelope said. "Let's begin spreading the word. Tell everyone you know, Sandy, we want as many people there as possible."

"Is there a budget?" Sandy asked. She hated talking numbers. It was one reason she didn't publicise that she could also do catering jobs; typically someone would come in and ask her for a price for a job, and she would calculate a fair price for her time and the supplies needed, only for the person to explain their disbelief that a few sandwiches could cost so much. With the cafe, her menu was displayed and anyone placing an order had already seen the price and was happy to pay it.

"Spend what you need to, and charge us fairly for your time. We don't want you to work the Ball, by the way, that's why we decided on a buffet. We want you and Bernice to come, as our special guests."

"I'm sure I can speak for us both and say that would be an honour."

"Oh, how exciting. I love to plan a party." Penelope said, then looked down at her jodhpurs and boots. "I must remember how to dress a tad smarter than this, though!"

"And me smarter than this." Sandy agreed, looking down at her apron. It had been a long time since she had

had an occasion to dress for. The thought of trying on clothes filled her with dread. Any incident involving her and a dressing room usually ended badly.

"The whole village together, it will be marvellous." Benedict said, with a faraway smile. He was in his element when doing things for the village that his family had called home for several generations. The manor was not his, not really, he was trusted to look after it until it passed to his heir. The fortune was similar; his, but not really.

"Will Charlotte and Sebastian be there?" Sandy asked. Charlotte returned home frequently, and even more often than usual lately, but Sebastian had been travelling the world on a gap year for the last three years and hadn't returned once.

"Charlotte will be," Penelope said. "Sebastian is in Africa. He's spending a few months on a project to build schools out there."

"How amazing," Sandy said. She liked Sebastian and hoped he returned to the village at some point.

"He has an Instagram," Benedict said, pronouncing the word as if it was a second language. "I don't know quite what that means but the housekeeper shows me photographs on the computer of what he's up to."

"It must be the trip of a lifetime," Sandy said, although she thought that if she had taken a year out at Sebastian's age she wouldn't have had anywhere near enough confidence to travel around the world on her own. She admired him for it.

"Yes, it is," Penelope said. "All good things must end at some point, though. He knows that this is his future. When we hand things over."

"Oh." Sandy said. "Will it not be Charlotte who takes over?"

"She has no interest in living a public life." Benedict said. He often spoke of his life in that way, as though he were a performer and the village was his audience. It was a commitment he took seriously.

The Harlow name was an honour to carry.

14

*S*andy made the drive to the next town early the
morning after her talk with the Harlows. Bernice
had accepted the short notice offer of extra hours as they
prepared for the Winter Ball, and was opening the shop and
preparing the day's cakes while Sandy made the run to the
wholesalers.

It was a crisp but bitter cold day, with a misleading
bright sun. Sandy felt foolish driving in her sunglasses and
mac, but the car was old and the heating was unreliable. It
seemed to be able to either chill the car to a comfortable -5,
or warm the interior to a toasty 100 degrees, and nothing in
between. Buying a new second-hand car was on Sandy's list
of things to do, as soon as there was more money coming in.

She didn't visit the wholesaler often, opting instead for a
regular weekly delivery that saved her time, and there was
no welcome when she walked through the doors.

The Harlows wanted a buffet, but it needed to be an
impressive buffet. Cheese and pineapple on sticks wouldn't
cut it.

Sandy had worked late the night before creating a buffet menu and was excited to get to work on it.

She wandered the wholesalers filling a trolley with plates, cutlery, and platters. She had some, but not enough.

Next, she picked up seven bags of arborio rice, a large bag of sundried tomatoes, two packets of dried porcini mushrooms and four bulbs of garlic. The mini risotto was an ambitious addition to the menu, but if she could cook it to perfection and then keep it warm and moist until serving, she knew it would be a crowd pleaser.

She added a large jar of queen olives to the trolley and three packets of goat's cheese, plus a large bottle of balsamic vinegar, then moved through the aisles with reckless abandon. Being able to prepare a menu of her own creation, with no set budget, almost made her giddy.

She grabbed a huge bag of cheddar cheese, another bag of red Leicester, and four large spring onions. Next, she added a huge bag of potatoes to the trolley, followed by ten heads of broccoli and a wheel of Stilton. Three dozen eggs followed. Individual cheese and potato pies, and broccoli and stilton quichettes, were on her menu.

An hour and a half later, she left the wholesaler empty-handed, opting for the items to be delivered. The order total was more than a month's rent, but it would be worth it.

The heavens opened on her drive back to Books and Bakes, and Sandy turned the radio off so she could hear the rain hammer against her car. As she left the more built-up town and returned to Waterfell Tweed, she thought how glad she was to live in a small village. The sight of green fields always soothed her soul.

She was thoroughly relaxed until she saw a police car parked outside Books and Bakes.

She parked in front of it and jumped out, only to notice

that the engine was still on and DC Sullivan was sat inside. She glanced inside the shop, where Bernice was placing a large breakfast in front of Dorie Slaughter.

"Ms Shaw." DC Sullivan said, lowering his car window. He had such an unpleasant face, Sandy thought. So arrogant and smug.

"DC Sullivan. Is everything ok?"

"No. No it isn't." The man said, sneering at her. Sandy's heart sank; what had happened now?

He noticed her expression and rolled his eyes. Actually rolled his eyes. "There's a murderer walking the streets. A murderer who should be in jail."

As if she had forgotten. "Of course, officer. Do you have any new leads?"

"I don't need any new leads." He grunted. "I know exactly who did this, and I want to be clear with you Ms. Shaw, I have worked on bigger and better cases than this, and I have caught bigger and cleverer criminals than you. Your days are numbered. I assure you, you will be punished."

With that, he sped away, leaving Sandy standing on the pavement, her cheeks burning with anger and fear, attempting not to cry.

She glanced from side to side to ensure that nobody else had heard the conversation, then walked away from the shop and into the pub. Finding the quietest booth in the empty pub, she sat and tried to calm her breathing, then took out her phone.

"Ingrid?" She asked when the woman answered the phone on the sixth ring.

"Ingrid Tate, who's calling?"

"It's Sandy Shaw."

"Sandy...?"

"Sandy Shaw. You represented me at the police station, do you remember."

"Of course!" The lawyer said, unconvincingly. "Have you been arrested again?"

"No!" Sandy cried. "No! I wanted to know what's happened, what's happened since the interview."

"Well, nothing's happened," Ingrid said.

"What do you mean? I thought you were on my side?"

"I was, Sandy. I was at the police station, I got you bail. But there's nothing to do now."

"So I sit back and wait to be charged?"

"Well... there really isn't anything else to do."

"Thanks for your help," Sandy said, her voice dripping with sarcasm. She had no knowledge of the legal world, no idea whether her so-called solicitor was any good and even less idea what she thought the solicitor should have been doing instead of doing nothing. But she knew she felt alone. Alone and scared.

**

"Get everything we need?" Bernice asked as Sandy returned to Books and Bakes after composing herself with an apple juice in The Tweed.

She nodded, not quite ready for Bernice's enthusiasm. Bernice had been suggesting to her for a long time that they should try and work more corporate catering occasions, but Sandy wasn't so sure. They were enjoyable every so often, a nice chance to work under pressure which always gave her a buzz of excitement, but customers usually wanted high-quality food for low prices. It was too much work to do without making a fair profit. Luckily, the Harlows appreciated that and always paid a fair amount.

"You're miles away. I bet you're still tweaking the menu!" Bernice said, with a grin.

"I haven't decided what cakes to make yet," Sandy said. "In fact, I thought maybe you could be in charge of that side of things?"

"What, choose the cakes myself?"

"You know what people like," Sandy said, with a shrug.

Bernice was beaming, her smile so wide it reached her eyes. "I'd love to."

Sandy smiled at her, forcing herself to focus on the good. She had a great event to cater, and a great employee to help her.

She pulled her apron on and got back to work, just as Elaine Peters walked in the door.

"Good afternoon, Elaine." Sandy greeted.

"Hello, Sandy, I can't stay but I wanted to tell you something. Can I have a word?"

"Of course," Sandy said, leading Elaine to a quiet corner of the deserted book area. "What's wrong?"

Elaine looked close to tears. "I've just had a visit from DC Sullivan."

"What did he want?"

"He asked me questions... about you. Said it was just informal, no need to go to the station. I didn't know what to do, I mean you can't refuse to talk to a police officer, can you? So I let him in but I didn't like it, Sandy. I didn't like his questions."

"It's fine, Elaine. I've got nothing to hide, you've done nothing wrong."

"He said something to me, and I think you deserve to know."

"Ok... what was it?"

"He told me he's got enough evidence to charge you, he's

just waiting for the right time. He said after the way you've been parading around town - they're his words, not mine - after the way you've been parading around town, he wants everyone to know what you did. And then he said he's looking forward to the Winter Ball."

Sandy creased her brow. Why would DC Sullivan be at the Winter Ball?

"Why would DC Sullivan be at the Winter Ball?"

"He said he's had a personal invitation, which I thought was strange because Jim... Jim hasn't." Elaine said, blushing at the mention of her boyfriend's name. "Nobody's had an invitation."

Sandy nodded. Whenever the Harlows hosted an event, it was announced and everyone was welcome, but there was no formal guest list and no individual invitations. The Harlows refused to do that in case someone was missed out. "Thanks for telling me, Elaine."

She bid her friend goodbye, then returned to the kitchen and took out her notebook.

WHO INVITED DC SULLIVAN? She wrote in large letters, as she tried to work out exactly what might lay in store for her at the Winter Ball.

15

*S*andy wrapped her mac tighter around herself as she walked up the gravel path to Waterfell Manor. The stately home sat in an elevated position, overlooking much of the village. It was a beautiful old building, maintained by the many generations of the Harlow family who had inhabited it before passing it to the next generation.

Sandy had no memory of the manor being home to anyone but Benedict and Penelope, but the entrance hall to the Manor was filled with oil paintings of the earlier inhabitants, who had each taken their turn managing and protecting the Harlow home and fortune.

She knocked on the door and stood back to wait for an answer. After a few moments, she heard someone approaching from within. To her surprise, Charlotte Harlow opened the door. Dressed in jodhpurs and a checked shirt, Charlotte's expression was sullen.

"Yes?" She asked, inconvenienced by having to answer the door herself. Sandy wondered where the housekeeper was.

"Are your parents in?" Sandy asked, the words making

her feel as if she was talking to a child and not a woman the same age as herself. Despite her moving to the city to embark on her own career, whenever Charlotte returned home, she seemed childlike again, living in her parents' shadow.

"Mother!" Charlotte called, walking away from the door but leaving it open. Sandy followed Charlotte inside, closing the door after herself.

"It's such a beautiful home." She mumbled, to herself as much as Charlotte.

"It's too big, impossible to heat, and the windows are tiny," Charlotte said. "What do you want, anyway?"

"I wanted to have a look at the kitchen. I'll be preparing the food here for the Ball, and I wanted to see what I need to bring and just look at the space where I'll be working."

Charlotte nodded. "Mother! The woman from the cafe is here!"

"You know my name," Sandy said, her cheeks burning with rage at Charlotte's rudeness.

"Do I?" Charlotte asked, and with that, she turned on her heels and left Sandy standing in the entrance way alone.

She remained there for several minutes, and then heard movement towards the end of the hall.

"Hello?" She called, feeling spooked by the size of the Manor and wondering if Charlotte was right. "Hello? It's Sandy Shaw, can you hear me?"

"Sandy!" Penelope called, appearing from a doorway in a body warmer and an old pair of jeans. Her hands, and spots of her face covered in soil. "So sorry darling, I was in the garden. Won't kiss you!"

Sandy smiled. "That's ok. I just wondered if I could have a look at the kitchen? I like to check out a space before I cook in it."

"Oh! What a professional thing to think of doing! Yes, yes, follow me."

Sandy followed Penelope through the Manor, down a long hallway. The kitchen was right at the end, and it was even more incredible than Sandy remembered. The island in the middle felt bigger than Sandy's home, and she couldn't wait to use the Aga that stood against one wall.

"What a beautiful space," Sandy said.

Penelope shrugged. "I can't say I come in here. The garden, that's more my type of space."

"What have you been doing out there?" Sandy asked, surprised to find that her wealthiest neighbour had such a mundane hobby.

"I've got a little vegetable garden, follow me," Penelope said, and Sandy did so.

The little vegetable garden was bigger than Sandy's whole garden, and it was beautifully tended. Vegetables and herbs grew in neat rows, each labelled to reveal what was busy growing there. Behind the vegetables was a manicured lawn, complete with a rusted slide and a large wooden climbing frame.

This garden was separate from the public gardens that surrounded the Manor. This was the family garden.

"I can see why you'd rather be out here than in the kitchen," Sandy admitted, picturing herself sitting out in the tranquil space in the summer reading a book.

"I'd spend entire days out here when the children were small," Penelope said with a smile.

"It must be a wonderful place to grow up."

"I hope so," Penelope said. "We tried to make it that way. They both grew up and left though, didn't they."

The two stood together in silence for a while, each one lost in their thoughts. Sandy was remembering her own childhood, how idyllic it had been growing up in a small village where everyone knew everyone and her safety was taken for granted.

She remembered running off to the grocery store or the newsagent to fetch things for her parents, saying hello to everyone she passed on the way. Sometimes, elderly women would stop her and dig in their purse to give her 20p for sweets.

Then there were the days she and Coral would disappear after breakfast and only return for dinner, worn out and golden brown from a day playing in the sun. She smiled at the thoughts.

"Shall we get to work?" Penelope asked, bringing Sandy back to reality.

"Yes, let's."

They returned to the kitchen and Sandy began checking drawers and cupboards for equipment and tools she would need. As expected, the Harlow kitchen had everything she would need. It was a kitchen designed for professionals since the family themselves didn't cook. On a typical night, the housekeeper would make dinner, and when guests were over, often a professional chef would be hired.

"This is perfect, Penelope, it will be a great space to work in," Sandy said. Penelope had hovered in the room, as if she may be called upon to answer a question while knowing that if that happened she wouldn't know the answer. It was the way Sandy felt whenever she had to call a plumber out or see a mechanic.

"Oh, I'm so pleased!" She said. "The Winter Ball will be just what we all need."

There came a loud crash from upstairs and Penelope glanced at the ceiling, then across at Sandy, who tried to act as though she hadn't heard.

"Charlotte's up there doing something or other," Penelope said, with a smile.

"She wants to move back, doesn't she?" Sandy asked, thinking back to the comment she overheard at the wake.

"Oh, yes. She'd do anything for a quiet life."

**

Sandy had one more visit to make.

Her relationship with Cass had been strained since she'd overheard the argument in the village square. While she knew that Cass' attack meant she couldn't have been responsible for Reginald's murder, and she was horrified that she had ever considered her best friend to be a suspect, she had a troubling feeling that Cass may know something. That she may not have been responsible, but involved with the wrong people at the wrong time.

She opened the door to Cass' salon, to find her friend just taking money from a customer with furious, red eyebrows. The woman thanked her and left the salon, and it was just Sandy and Cass.

"Hey, you!" Cass said with a grin. She was sporting an oversized green dress with large white spots, black tights, and black boots. The outfit would look garish on Sandy, but Cass pulled it off with style.

"Hey, I love that dress on you."

"Hides the bumps and lumps!" Cass said with a laugh, giving Sandy a hug. "I've got a break until 2pm, want a coffee?"

"Please." Sandy said. "And can you fit me in for that eyebrow wax?"

Cass' eyes glinted with excitement. "Ohhhh yes! Come and lie on here."

Sandy lay down on the treatment bed and closed her eyes. The wax was warm, which she knew it would be but was still surprised to feel. It felt thick and sticky, but the sensation of it being applied was soothing.

"Get ready." Cass said, applying some kind of sticky tape on top of part of the wax, rubbing it, and then tearing it off.

"Ow! Cass! Am I bleeding?!" Sandy cried, sitting up on the bed and placing a hand on her hurt eyebrow, coating her fingers with wax.

Cass laughed. "Come on, Sand, it's not that bad. Lie back down, you're nearly done."

Sandy lay down, wiping the wax on a wet wipe offered by Cass. She remained lying down for the rest of the treatment, and a few minutes later glanced in the mirror to see her own red, angry, but tidy, eyebrows.

"Thanks, I guess," Sandy said, as she and Cass sat with a cup of coffee afterward. "How do people put up with that?"

"Lots of people prefer it to plucking," Cass explained. "I don't think it hurts once you get used to it. And look how nice and tidy your eyebrows look nice."

"They do look nice," Sandy admitted.

"Well, pop in anytime. It's only five minutes."

"Thanks Cass. You know, there's something I've been wanting to ask you about for a few days."

Cass shifted in her seat. "Okay... what is it?"

"A few nights ago, I was followed by a man on my walk home from the shop."

"What? Are you okay? Do the police know?"

"It was the police."

"You are kidding me."

"No, it was DC Sullivan. In fairness, he did it because he didn't want me walking home on my own after the murder, but I only found out it was him the next day. The night it happened, I just turned and ran. And I ran back to the shop. I slept there."

"Oh, wow."

"I know. The beanbags really aren't that comfortable after a while." She said with a smile. "The thing is, though, when I was in the shop that night, I heard something. I heard you. You were arguing with someone. And I know you don't have to tell me everything, but you don't argue with people and not tell me. I'm worried about you, Cass."

The colour had drained from Cass' face. She looked at the floor and tapped her feet rhythmically.

"What's wrong, Cass?"

Cass took a deep breath and looked up at Sandy. "I'm hiding something."

Sandy reached over and took her friend's hand in hers. "You can tell me anything."

"If I tell you, you'll tell the police."

"Why would I tell the police?"

"Because I've broken the law, Sandy. I'm in so much trouble."

And with that, Cass began to cry. Sandy pulled her in for a hug, then noticed a shadow standing by the door to the kitchen.

"Cass, who's that?" Sandy asked.

Cass jumped up from her seat and looked at the kitchen, noticing the shadow for herself. "I told you to stay there!"

The door opened, and a small teenage girl appeared. She was short, painfully thin, and sporting bruises across her arm and face.

"What's going on, Cass?" Sandy asked.

Cass sighed and buried her head in her hands. "Sandy, this is Olivia. My sister."

"You don't have a sister," Sandy said. She had known

Cass since they were children, there had never been another child in the Zuniper house.

"Half-sister." The girl said, her voice sullen.

"My dad had an affair," Cass said. "My mum knew, she told him that he had to choose, and he chose us. But he didn't tell us he had another daughter."

"Why didn't you tell me?"

"Olivia turned up two nights before Reginald's murder. I didn't want a new face in the village then, she would have been the first suspect. And she had nothing to do with it, she just arrived at the wrong time."

"I heard you say you'd lied."

"I did."

"What about?" Sandy asked, an uncomfortable feeling settling in her stomach.

"Reginald was taking over my shop, Sandy. I lied to you about that."

"Why?"

"He came to me and offered me a great deal, a big payout if I agreed. I was only convinced because of Olivia. Look at the state of her, Sand. I can't send her home. She came empty handed and I don't have money to get her new clothes and everything she'll need. It was like Reginald was psychic, he turned up the night Olivia had, with his offer. I said yes straight away. But then he was killed, and I had to hide Olivia. I couldn't tell you he was taking the shop, I knew you'd want to know why."

"But there's no official paper trail showing that he was taking over here."

"I can't explain that, the process was definitely set in motion. I lied before, I'm not lying now."

"I believe you," Sandy said, gripping her hand.

"Olivia, come out here," Cass said. The girl did. She

looked so vulnerable, it broke Sandy's heart. "Meet my oldest friend in the world, Sandy."

"I'm not that old." Sandy teased, but Olivia didn't react.

"Please don't go to the police," Cass whispered.

"Why would I?"

"She's only 15. She ran away from home to find me."

"Oh, Cass. We need to tell the police. Her mum will be worried sick."

"My mum's never cared!" Olivia said, crossing her arms.

"She was in foster care, Sand. Removed from her mum when she was six."

The thought of a child being removed from the only parent she knew at such a young age made Sandy's stomach wince with pain. What must this poor girl have been through in her short life?

"What's your plan?" Sandy asked Cass.

"She stays here. I'm the only family she's got, she has to stay here."

"Then you need to do things properly. You can't hide her away, Cass, if you do that they won't let her stay when they do find her here."

"And how are they going to find me? Are you going to tell them?" Olivia asked, but her tone then was not aggressive. It was her real voice, under the act. The voice of a scared child.

"No," Sandy said. "That's not my place. I will do something though, give me ten minutes."

She stood up and left the salon, running across the village green. She burst into Books and Bakes, greeting the familiar customers and giving Bernice a hug.

"What was that for?" Bernice asked with a laugh.

"I just remembered how lucky I am to have you," Sandy said. She went straight into the kitchen and grabbed a cake box, then filled it with a slice of each cake she had. Coffee and walnut, hazelnut torte, Victoria sponge, a slice of flapjack, two cherry Bakewells, and an enormous elephant's foot cream cake. Satisfied, she placed the lid on the box and dashed out of the shop again, leaving a confused Bernice watching after her.

When she got back to the salon, Cass and Olivia were sitting in the back together, holding hands. They both looked up when Sandy raced in.

"I bring cake." She announced, handing the cake box to Olivia.

"Wow." The girl said, then looked up at Sandy. "Are these all for me?"

"Absolutely," Sandy said. To her delight, Olivia picked up the elephant's foot straight away and took a huge bite, cream spilling all down her chin.

Cass pulled Sandy to one side, leaving her sister to work her way through the cream cake.

"I'm so sorry I lied to you." She said.

"It's done now, Cass. Don't worry."

"Will you keep our secret? I know I can't ask you that, but I have no choice. I'm all she's got."

"I won't tell the police," Sandy said. "I'm going to catch the real killer, and then you can tell the police yourself."

16

"*I*t smells amazing in here!" Coral said, appearing in the kitchen of Books and Bakes as Sandy and Bernice made the finishing touches to the food they had prepared ahead of time.

The Manor kitchen would be the venue for most of the baking and food preparation, but there was so much to do, Sandy had suggested they do at least some the day before in their own kitchen. As cramped as the space was compared to the Manor kitchen, it was a space they were familiar with, and that made them work faster.

In what felt like no time at all, they had measured and chopped ingredients, arranged all of the serving platters and dishes they would need, and baked four large cakes.

Coral was right, the smell was incredible.

"You've not come to lend a hand, have you?" Bernice asked, pulling the twice-baked strawberry shortcake cheese-cake out of the oven.

"Panic not!" Coral said with a laugh. "I just thought I'd offer to walk you home, Sand, if you're nearly done."

"I won't be much longer," Sandy said. "You could make a start on the washing up if you want to help?"

Coral rolled her eyes. "Go on then. I must be mad - I could have sat and waited in The Tweed."

She busied herself at the sink, though, and Sandy was grateful. The job of clearing up after a busy day was always the worst job to do at night but the one you were most grateful you had done when you returned the next morning.

"This boozy trifle smells strong enough to get you drunk," Bernice said, opening the fridge door. The seasonal, and very boozy, trifle had been Sandy's idea. Alcohol made everyone lose their inhibitions, and she thought that might come in handy at the Ball.

"Let's have a sniff," Coral said, moving away from the sink and standing next to Bernice. "Wowzers! What's in it?"

"It's a mulled wine jelly with an advocaat custard," Sandy said, wondering if she had overdone the alcohol in it. She hadn't followed a recipe, but had just added a few slugs and used her own taste buds to decide when to stop.

"I'll be giving that a try tomorrow," Coral said. "Sounds fab!"

"I hope they like everything," Sandy said. She always felt nervous as an important catering day grew nearer, and she particularly wanted Penelope and Benedict Harlow to be happy with her work.

"They'll love it all, you watch," Bernice reassured, giving Sandy's arm a squeeze. "Why don't you two get off home? I can finish up here."

"Oh, no, I couldn't..." Sandy began.

"We totally could. Come on, Sandy, you need to learn to let people do things for you. Let's leave Bernice to it."

"Are you sure?" Sandy asked, wondering how she got so lucky to have such a generous friend and employee.

"Absolutely. All I'll do when I get home is watch trash TV, that can wait a while longer."

Sandy beamed at her. "Thank you."

**

"So, what's this visit for?" Sandy asked as they walked together to her cottage. Coral linked her arm in Sandy's and snuggled in close. It was a bitter cold evening and the famous Waterfell Tweed wind was blowing.

"I just had a rubbish day at work, and nobody makes me feel better like my little sister does."

"You tell me who upset you and I'll sort them." Sandy joked.

"Nobody upset me," Coral said. "But things have changed there. Do you remember me telling you my boss was ill?"

"I think so," Sandy said. "Was it cancer?"

"I don't know, we were never told the details. But he just became less visible. He was working from home a lot, and people talked as people do, but all we were really told was that he was poorly."

"Yep, I think I do remember," Sandy said. The Waterfell Way had been run for decades by the son of the gentleman who had started the paper. It was a small, close-knit team. Sandy was asked to bake cakes whenever it was a member of staff's birthday, and when she made the deliveries it always struck her how cosy and homely the newspaper offices seemed.

"Well, there was a big meeting today and I thought the news would be that he had passed the running of the paper to his son, but it turns out we've been bought by a national news agency."

"Woah... what does that mean?" Sandy asked. Selling out to a national company wasn't the Waterfell Tweed way. Almost every business in the village was independent. This was big news.

"Nobody knows. There will be more meetings, but the first change they've introduced is time cards."

"Time cards? Are you working in a factory now?"

"It feels that way. Stamping in and out, as if I've been pretending to be at work all these years and can't be trusted. It's insulting."

"Oh, sis. What a mess. Well, I'm sure it will settle down. The national company will want one of you guys to run things, surely as soon as they decide who that is, things will get back to normal?"

"Yeah, I'm sure you're right," Coral said, giving Sandy's arm a squeeze. "Has the shop been getting any busier?"

The winter months were the quietest time for Sandy, as even the most determined walkers didn't spend their free time rambling in the countryside any more, and the business from the regular locals wasn't enough.

"No, but I've got a plan," Sandy admitted.

"You've always got a plan." Coral teased, which was true. "That's what losing our mum did for us."

"Do you think?" Sandy asked. She had never connected losing her mum young in life with her tendency to want to take control and sort things out. Like solving the murder - it wasn't her job, but she'd decided she would do it.

"Absolutely. I've interviewed lots of strong women and usually, they lost someone important when they were young."

"I'd hardly call myself a strong woman," Sandy said.

Coral shrugged. "Maybe you're just bossy, then."

Sandy laughed. They reached her cottage and she

unlocked the door and turned the light on in the passage.
They kicked their shoes off and Sandy made them both a big mug of hot chocolate, even adding marshmallows and whipped cream.

"Wow!" Coral said as Sandy walked into the living room with the two cups. "Now that's a hot chocolate!"

The sisters sat in silence for a while, each enjoying the warmth of their drink after the cold wind outside.

Sandy had waited for the right time but knew she could wait no longer.

"Coral." She said, and her tone of voice made her sister look at her in concern. "I know who the killer is."

17

*S*andy was up early the next morning.

She dressed in her favourite pair of jeans, her baggy 'I Love Waterfell Tweed' t-shirt and a pair of ballet pumps. Comfort was the main requirement on a big catering day.

She needed the day to go well, and once it was over, she was going to see DC Sullivan to tell him who the real killer was. The thought made the insides of her stomach flip with nerves.

She drove to the Manor to see Bernice's car already parked on the gravel. As Sandy locked her car door, Bernice appeared from the house to fetch more things from the car.

"Morning." She called, opening the car boot.

"Morning, sorry I'm late," Sandy said.

"You're not late, I was early. The wind woke me up. May as well be here getting a head start if I'm up anyway."

"I didn't hear any wind, must have slept through it," Sandy said. She was woken by the wind often but she also thought she had got used to the noises of where she lived, as she imagined people in the city must get used to police sirens without panicking each time.

"Lucky for some," Bernice said with a smile. She looked tired, Sandy noticed for the first time.

"Here, let me get some of those," Sandy said, as Bernice attempted to carry a huge tower of empty platters.

"I'm ok, you get some of the others." Bernice insisted.

Sandy grabbed another pile and then they walked together back to the manor.

The kitchen was cold and Sandy wished she'd brought a cardigan with her, although she knew she would warm up as soon as she got to work.

"Are the Harlows around?" Sandy asked.

"I haven't seen them. The housekeeper let me in."

One more trip to the car was all they needed to bring everything into the kitchen. They washed their hands and turned on the radio that stood on one of the kitchen counters.

They had six hours to prepare everything before people arrived. It was a stretch, but they would do it. Both Sandy and Bernice worked well under pressure.

**

By the time it was 1.30pm, the kitchen was overflowing with the dishes they had created. Sandy stood back to admire it all.

"We're a good team!" She exclaimed.

Bernice followed her eye and burst into a grin. "It's so satisfying to see a job like this done, isn't it."

"It certainly is!" A booming voice came from behind them. Sandy turned to see Benedict Harlow standing in the kitchen doorway, admiring the food. Penelope stood by his side.

"You two have outdone yourselves," Penelope said.

"Thank you." Sandy and Bernice said in unison.

"Now, go on upstairs both of you. I had to guess your sizes but I'm hopeful I have them right. I got a dress for each of you to wear, as a little thank you." Penelope said.

"What?" Sandy said, in shock. "We're going to hand the food out, we'll be..."

"Oh no, I couldn't ask you to do that and not enjoy the Ball for yourselves. I've hired some college students from the next town to do all of that and the washing up, so you ladies can enjoy yourselves."

"Wow! That's amazing!" Bernice said.

"Follow me." Penelope said, and Sandy and Bernice were whisked out of the kitchen and up the grand staircase.

"The manor is so beautiful," Bernice said, taking in all of the details as they walked down a wood-panelled passageway.

"Why, thank you," Penelope said as if she had never heard the compliment before. They stopped walking when they reached a particular door. "This is your room, Sandy. Bernice, you're the next one there. Now leave your belongings in here nobody will be inside here, and then you can get changed again later."

"Thank you, Penelope. This is a really kind thing to do." Sandy said, opening the door to reveal a large guest bedroom with a four-poster bed and a view of the gardens. A huge marquee stood proud on the grounds, ready to hold the Ball.

Lying on the bed was a floor-length blue velvet dress. It was beautiful.

Sandy approached it and ran her hand down the material. She had never worn a dress like it in her life.

She sat on the bed and looked out of the window. People had already arrived and were milling around on the lawn, accepting glasses of champagne from the college waiters. Sandy could see her sister and Cass, standing together and talking. Cass looked up suddenly, right at Sandy as if she had felt her eyes on her. She smiled and waved, and Sandy did the same, then moved away from the window.

As she did so, she sensed a movement in the room and felt her heart race. "Bernice?"

Silence.

Sandy let out a small laugh, then sat herself down on the stool in front of the vanity table. She was just about to pull her hair out of its ponytail when there was a knock at the door.

"Come in." She called.

To her surprise, Charlotte Harlow appeared in the doorway. "Mother asked me to bring you a drink."

She walked across to Sandy and placed a glass of champagne on the vanity table.

"Thanks, Charlotte," Sandy said. "Oh, can you tell me where the nearest toilet is in here?"

Charlotte scowled at her. "It's next door, to the left."

"I thought that was the room Bernice is getting ready in?" Sandy said, more to herself than Charlotte.

"It's this room, then the bathroom, then the other bedroom. Make sure you don't take too long, the party is about to start." Charlotte said, with a smile that dripped insincerity, then she left the room.

Sandy waited for Charlotte to close the door behind her, then she picked up the dress and the champagne glass, and went into the bathroom.

**

She emerged minutes later, feeling less self-conscious than she thought she would in such a dress. Penelope had guessed her size correctly, and even picked a style that Sandy appreciated. A ruched panel across the stomach area hid her wobbly belly, and she was very pleased that the dress had sleeves as she hated her bare arms.

She stood at the top of the staircase, getting her composure.

"Shall we?" Bernice asked.

Sandy turned to see her friend. She was wearing a floor-length red dress that hugged her slender figure in all the right places and hid that her bosom was fairly modest. Penelope should be a professional dresser!

"Oh my, you look incredible."

"You look beautiful!"

The women gushed over each other. They were used to seeing each other in aprons and comfortable clothes.

They descended the staircase hand in hand, giggling as they did. The inside of the manor was bustling with activity as the waiters moved trays of food and drinks outside and trays of empty glasses back inside.

Outside, flooring had been laid on the grass so guests didn't have to get wet or muddy feet. Sandy and Bernice followed the path they made to the marquee, where hundreds of people were standing chatting, sitting eating, or dancing to the DJ who was set up at the far end.

There was a heavy police presence and Sandy caught the gaze of DC Sullivan, who stood near the marquee entrance in full uniform. He held her gaze without a smile.

A stage stood at the left-hand side of the long marquee,

and as Sandy and Bernice reached Coral and Cass and joined their table, Penelope and Benedict Harlow took to the stage.

"Ladies and gentlemen!" Benedict boomed into a microphone. "If we could have your attention for one moment, my wife and I would like to welcome you all to the first annual Waterfell Tweed Winter Ball."

A round of applause spread through the room, and Sandy felt a rush of affection as she scanned the crowds and saw familiar faces dressed their best for the occasion.

She might have bought her favourite t-shirt to help raise money, but the words on it were true. She really loved Waterfell Tweed.

"We hope you will enjoy today. Please join us in a round of applause for Sandy and Bernice from Books and Bakes, who have made this delicious food."

The crowd clapped and the people nearby raised their glasses to Sandy and Bernice and mouthed 'thank you' to them.

"The mini quiche is to die for!" A voice that sounded very much like Dorie Slaughter's called across the room as the clapping stopped. Everyone laughed.

"A round of applause for our hard-working team serving you today," Penelope said into the microphone. "And a round of applause for our fabulous DJ, who will be accepting requests to get you all up on the dancefloor this afternoon."

"And finally," Benedict said, sensing that the crowd was becoming restless. People were at the Ball to eat, drink and be merry, not listen to speeches. "May today remind us all that, despite recent events, there truly is no place like Waterfell Tweed. Happy Winter Ball!"

The crowd cheered for that point, clapping hands or

stamping feet if their hands were full of food and drink. An impromptu round of 'three cheers for Waterfell Tweed' was started by someone, and Sandy felt her eyes water.

"Are you ok?" Cass asked her.

Sandy nodded. "It's all making me emotional."

"Yeah, I know what you mean," Cass said. "The Harlows know how to bring the community together, don't they."

Sandy felt a lump in her throat and nodded. "I'm just going to go to the toilet."

She walked out of the marquee as quickly as she could, fighting through the throngs of people who were still cheering for the village in between bites of her food. She darted inside the manor and raced up the staircase, heading back to the room where she had got ready.

Sitting on the bed, she covered her face with her hands and tried to calm her breathing.

She wasn't surprised when she heard the door open.

"Charlotte." She said, without looking up.

"Are you ill?" The woman asked, closing the door behind her.

Sandy opened her eyes and stood up, trying to keep a distance between the two of them. "Why did you do it?"

Charlotte laughed. "Why did I do what?"

"Why did you kill Reginald? Why did you try to kill me?"

"Oh, Sandy... you think you've got it all figured out?" Charlotte asked. She stood with her back against the door, blocking Sandy's exit.

"I know it's the bookshops, but I don't understand why." Sandy said, forcing herself to wobble as she moved. Appearing ill was her only way of surviving this confrontation.

Charlotte noticed the wobble and smiled. "You should

sit down, you look quite ill. I'll fetch mother shortly. But not yet."

"Charlotte..." Sandy said, stumbling to the bed.

"Sit down and I'll tell you a story," Charlotte said, moving away from the door. She sat down on the vanity desk stool. "The second bookshop should never have been Reginald's. I gave him the idea. I thought - ha - I thought for a moment we were similar, and I told him my plan."

"To move back here?"

"To move back here and put you out of business." Charlotte spat.

"You could have done that easily, Charlotte. You've got money and connections. You didn't need to hurt anyone."

"I couldn't let that fool open my business and have everyone imagine it had been his idea. What could I have done then? If I'd opened my business, people would have thought I'd copied Reginald Halfman! The insanity of it! I had to stop him."

"And once you'd stopped him..."

"I might as well stop you too. Exactly." Charlotte admitted. "Your friend messed that up, but it's quite a nice twist that you're under investigation. It didn't matter to me whether you were dead or in prison, to be blunt."

"So, you'll let me take the blame for what you did?" Sandy asked.

Charlotte laughed. "I would have done, of course! But the police are no better than Reginald. I'm surrounded by fools. DC Sullivan should have charged you straight away. I can't trust him to do the job properly. He hasn't even found any CCTV."

"You invited him today, didn't you? You gave him a personal invitation - why?"

Charlotte's face blanched. "Why would a murderer

invite a police officer to the scene of her next crime? My inviting him here today means I can't possibly be responsible for what will happen."

"What will happen, Charlotte?" Sandy asked, although she already knew the answer. Her breathing was more laboured, her eyelids heavy.

"It's already happened," Charlotte said, standing up and walking back towards the door. "There's been another poisoning. Awful business, really."

"Charlotte, please..." Sandy whispered.

"I'd better get back to the Ball. I'm sure someone will miss you, soon. Sweet dreams, Sandy." Charlotte said, opening the bedroom door. She turned to give Sandy one last glance, smirked, then left the room, leaving the door open.

"I didn't drink the champagne." Sandy whispered after she had gone, then sat up and stopped her phone recording. She sent the recording to Jim Slaughter and DC Sullivan and watched from the bedroom window a few minutes later as DC Sullivan approached Charlotte, who was standing in the doorway of the marquee downing a glass of champagne.

She watched as Charlotte attempted to laugh at whatever DC Sullivan said, then as her face grew red and finally paled of all colour as DC Sullivan presented handcuffs from his pocket and placed them on her.

Sandy moved away from the window as Charlotte was lead away.

"Sandy, are you ok?" Jim Slaughter called, running into the room. He was off duty and clearly quite tipsy. "We need to get you to hospital."

"I'm fine, Jim, I didn't drink any... I just pretended I had.

I knew she'd only admit what she'd done if she thought I was dying."

"But how were you so sure she had added something to your drink?"

"That woman has been horrible to me for as long as I've known her, Jim. There's only one reason she would bring me a glass of champagne as I got ready alone. And when I mentioned to Bernice how generous she had been bringing us a drink each, and Bernice told me she hadn't had one, I knew beyond doubt."

"I can't believe it." Jim said.

"I can believe it." Sandy said. "The woman has no remorse at all. But I can't understand it."

"I don't think we ever will." Jim said.

18

Sandy had debated whether to close Books and Bakes the day after Charlotte Harlow's arrest but had decided that the woman had caused enough destruction in the village already and shouldn't stop normal life for a moment longer.

As soon as the doors opened, she knew she had made the right decision. It felt like the whole village appeared at some point or another throughout the day.

To her surprise, Coral had appeared in the morning and offered to help.

"I felt like being close to you today." She had said, and while it was lovely to have her sister in the shop with her, Sandy thought there was more to it than that.

"If my son had been left in charge, this would have been sorted much earlier." Dorie Slaughter announced at frequent intervals throughout the day as she held court from her regular seat.

"I didn't realise your Jim had ever been in charge." Cass teased as she picked up a bacon sandwich each for herself and Olivia.

"Are you going to, you know, now?" Sandy asked discreetly.

"We're hoping this gives us some courage," Cass admitted. "I just hope they let her stay here. She's safe and warm and looked after."

"I'm sure they will," Sandy said. "There are plenty of kids in the system; surely if one of them can find a permanent home with a relative, that's best for everyone?"

"I hope so. Keep your fingers crossed for me!" She called. Sandy crossed her fingers and held her hand up to show it, as Cass left the shop and walked back across the village square. The idea of flighty, glamorous Cass with a sister to be responsible for would take some getting used to, but Sandy would do everything she could to help them both.

The door opened then and DC Sullivan walked in, causing the shop to fall silent.

"Hello, Detective Constable. I've got something for you." Sandy said, retreating into the kitchen. She reappeared with a cake box. She had made a chocolate fudge cake that morning and had planned to walk it over to the police station, where she was sure all of the officers would be busy with all of the work that catching a murderer required. "Chocolate fudge cake, fresh this morning."

To her surprise, the officer held his hands out and accepted the box. "Thank you, Sandy. I came to give you an apology. I was perhaps a little too, too aggressive in my focus on you. I'm sorry."

Sandy shrugged. "You were doing your job, I'm sure it was nothing personal."

"Trust me." DC Sullivan said with a laugh that revealed a dimple in his cheek. "I'd much rather have been in here eating cake with you than interviewing you at the station."

Sandy felt her cheeks flush. "Yes, yes, me too. And you're welcome anytime."

"I'll be back to city tomorrow, once the loose ends are tidied up. I'll need you to come and give a statement, but you can finish up here. Your recording paints a clear picture for us."

"I thought it might," Sandy said, feeling shame that the idea of recording a confrontation had first come to her when she believed that Elaine Peters had been the killer. How wrong she had been.

She bid farewell to DC Sullivan, and returned her attention to the shop. The customers were all sitting silently, listening to her conversation. She smiled. It was good to get back to normal village life, even if that included more gossiping than she'd like.

"Are you ok here?" Sandy asked Coral, who was doing a brilliant job of upgrading every order and making every customer spend more than they usually would have.

"Absolutely," Coral said, giving her sister a thumbs up.

Sandy went into the kitchen and dialled the familiar number. She held up the latest letter she'd received addressed to 'Sandy Shore'. She had been considering its offer for weeks and had realised that life was too short to have regrets.

"Mr Potter?" She asked as the old man answered with a barking cough.

"Who is this?" He managed, his breath rasping.

"It's Sandy Shaw." She said. "I've considered your offer and I'd like to accept; I would be very interested in extending and taking on the upstairs premises as well."

**

"Everything ok?" Coral asked as Sandy returned to the counter.

"Everything's better than okay. I've just extended the business. As from next week, I'll have the upstairs as well."

"That's amazing!" Coral said, giving her a warm hug.

"I'll be able to have a full floor for books," Sandy said. "I can specialise, I can really get the word out and attract people from further afield. I think it will be just what the shop needs."

She noticed Coral's eyes water and followed her hunch.

"You know, sis," Sandy said. "You're so good on the tills, you're a natural salesperson. Would you be interested in working here, properly?"

Coral began to cry. "Are you psychic?"

"I don't think so…" Sandy said, trying her best to feign ignorance.

"I just lost my job," Coral admitted. "The national company doesn't want us to carry on as we were at all, they just want to add the name to their list and run everything from London. The whole team has been made redundant."

"Oh, sis that's awful," Sandy said. "Perfect timing for Books and Bakes, though, hey?"

Coral eyed her sister and laughed.

"To the future?" Sandy suggested as Jim Slaughter and Elaine Peters walked in the shop hand-in-hand.

"To the future!" Coral agreed, giving her sister's hand a squeeze.

THANK YOU FOR READING

As an independent author, my success depends on readers sharing the word about my books and leaving honest reviews online.

If you enjoyed this book, please consider leaving an honest review on Amazon or GoodReads.

I know that your time is precious, and I am grateful that you chose to spend some of your time entering the world of Waterfell Tweed with me.

To keep up with the latest releases, visit:

http://monamarple.com/the-series/

ABOUT THE AUTHOR

Mona Marple is a mother, author and coffee enthusiast.

When she isn't busy writing a cozy mystery, she's probably curled up somewhere warm reading one.

She lives in the beautiful Peak District (where Waterfall Tweed is set in her imagination!) with her husband and daughter.

Connect with Mona:

www.MonaMarple.com

mona@monamarple.com

Made in the USA
Coppell, TX
02 September 2023

21095592R00094